RUNTIME

S. B. DIVYA

A TOM DOHERTY ASSOCIATES BOOK

NEW YORK

This is a work of fiction. All of the characters, organizations, and events portrayed in this novella are either products of the author's imagination or are used fictitiously.

RUNTIME

A Tor.com Book
Published by Tom Doherty Associates, LLC
175 Fifth Avenue
New York, NY 10010

www.tor.com

Tor® is a registered trademark of Tom Doherty Associates, LLC.

ISBN 978-0-7653-8978-7 (ebook)
ISBN 978-0-7653-8979-4 (trade paperback)

First Edition: May 2016

D 0 9 8 7 6 5 4 3 2

To everyone who has joined a group and felt like an outsider, in hopes that you will succeed where others desire your failure.

Acknowledgments

An astounding number of stars must align for a story to become a book. This being my first, I feel the urge to thank everyone who ever said a kind word about my writing—but that would turn into another book so I'll pare it down to the people who were essential to the existence of this one.

John Murphy and Vylar Kaftan, for the contest that motivated me to write a novella.

Dawn Bonanno, Brigitte McCray, Elizabeth Shack, and Darusha Wehm, for their comments and encouragement on the first draft.

Kathryn Eberle, Yasmin Malik, and Caroline M. Yoachim, for their insightful feedback on draft two.

Carl Engle-Laird, for loving this story and making it shine. Cameron McClure, for holding my hand as I navigated the world of publishing for the first time.

Daniel Marcus and Michaela Roessner, for their invaluable help in making me a better writer.

My daughter, Maya, for asking me to tell stories and stretch my creative muscles.

My husband, Ryan, for showing me that the best stories come from the riskiest ventures and for his unwavering support of my writing.

My parents, Anusha and Shaker, for babysitting, editing, and proofreading; for taking me on my first trip to the high Sierras; for life itself.

And last but not least, Manisha Gupta and Pushkala Venkatraman, my very first readers from nearly three decades ago, for asking me to send them the next chapter.

Runtime

The wall behind Marmeg thrummed with the muffled impact of bass beats. A line of girls in heels mixed with boys in lacy shirts, both interspersed with androgynous moots wearing whatever they wanted. Blue light spilled from the club's doorway onto cuffs and bracelets but mostly on bare skin.

The host was a moot with minimal curves of breast and hip, draped in a sheath of satin gray. Candy-colored red hair in two long curls framed zir face. This host wanted to be seen, and Marmeg had a hard time not looking.

Her own body tended toward her mother's build—no hiding the mammary glands and rounded buttocks. She mitigated it with the torso shell and a neutral haircut while dreaming of moot surgery.

Marmeg glanced at her cuff. Another twenty minutes until the end of her shift. The line drifted forward and two new people came into view. A nat male with waves of silky brown hair and a translucent suit stood near Marmeg, his gaze fixed on the screen in his hands.

"Unbelievable," he crowed. "Last round. Canter's

winning!"

His friend was a moot with a rainbow 'hawk and a bored expression.

"Fights? Last century much?" Zir red lips curled. "Races be where's at."

Zir friend looked up from his screen. "Minerva starts tomorrow."

Marmeg's heart pounded. The Minerva Sierra Challenge would be the first race of her life. She was a long shot with her outdated, refurbished embed gear, but one dark horse usually made it to the top five. She planned to be this year's surprise element.

"Be following that, sure," said Rainbow Hair. "Minerva's winner trumps the BP International."

"Not always. Two years ago, remember that? Topsy-turvy all over," the friend countered.

Their voices faded as the host let them in. Marmeg checked her cuff—fifteen more minutes—and shifted her weight. The host shot her a dirty look. Be invisible: that was Marmeg's role. Here at the club or out in the world, nobody wanted to see the likes of her, but she would be worth noticing soon.

The second-shift bouncers came out on time. Marmeg walked to the bus stop in full gear, drawing surprised glances from the small crowd waiting at the sign-post. A faint star forced its light past the competing glow of Los Angeles. Tomorrow night, she would be out in the middle of nothing and nowhere, and then she'd see more than one twinkle. *Star light, star bright, first and only star I see in this concrete clusterf—* The bus arrived.

She climbed in last and sat on a hard plastic chair. The screen above her displayed a white-haired Congressman next to a blonde talk-show host. Their voices blared through tinny speakers.

"US citizenship is a birthright. Voting is a birthright," the Congressman said. "But social services—public education, health care, retirement benefits—those need to be earned. Unlicensed families haven't paid into the system."

The blonde nodded. "Do you think we should repeal the Postnatal License Act?"

"The problem with postnatal licensing is the barrier to entry: it's too low. The unlicensed pay a small fee—that doesn't scale with age—and then they're like us."

"Bull," Marmeg muttered. She'd spent three years saving for her "small fee."

Her cuff zapped the skin on the inside of her wrist. She flicked it. The screen lit up and displayed a message from Jeffy.

SORRY TO BUG. SHIT'S GOING DOWN, HELP?

So much for getting a few hours of rest before catching the midnight bus to Fresno. Her brother needed rescuing more often than Marmeg cared to tally, especially right after a club shift. She hopped off the bus at the next stop and used Jeffy's cuff GPS to locate him: Long Beach.

She took the train to the station closest to her brother's location. From there, she ran in long, loping strides. Leg muscles encased by exoskeletons flexed and relaxed in a stronger, more graceful counterpoint than she could have achieved naturally. As she moved, she downloaded new code into the chips controlling her gear. She had developed the software to bypass the legal limits for her embeds. When it came to Jeffy's "friends," legal wasn't always good enough.

The fight house was a narrow single-story with a sagging wood porch that had been white at some point. Puddles of stale beer and vomit soaked into the weedy lawn. A cheerful roar rose from the backyard.

Marmeg ran along the right side of the house. A ring of people—mostly nats—blocked her view of the action. She crouched and sprang onto the roof, landing on all fours.

Jeffy reeled in the center of the crowd. Blood dripped from his nose and left ear. His black curls were plastered to his head by dripping sweat, one hank covering part of a swollen eye. His left leg had an obvious limp. Cords of muscle rippled under his torn shirt. Chestnut skin peeked through the hole.

Her brother hadn't done much after leaving the army, but he maintained a soldier's body. Not that it did him much good in these fights. His lithe opponent, clad in deteriorating exos, kicked him hard in the bad leg. It flew out from under him. He collapsed and lay unmoving.

The crowd cheered. Some of them waved bottles in the air. Others held old-fashioned paper money in their raised fists. Marmeg jumped into the clear center. The crowd roared again, probably expecting her to fight. Instead, she scooped up her unconscious brother, slung him over her shoulder, and leapt over the crowd. A disappointed groan rose from the onlookers. Marmeg barely heard it. She stumbled on her landing, Jeffy's bulk complicating her balance. She kept to a simple jog on the way to the bus station.

She paid for their bus fare with a swipe of her cuff. The orange-colored account balance glared from the screen. The extra cost to rescue her brother was unexpected, but she had enough money to buy her ticket to Fresno, barely.

"Can walk," Jeffy slurred when they were a few blocks from home.

Fine, let him arrive on his own two feet. He wouldn't be fooling anybody. Marmeg's cuff said it was slightly past ten o'clock, so the boys would be sleeping. That was a small mercy.

They walked in with Jeffy leaning heavily on her shoulder. She hardly felt his weight, but their mother's gaze landed like a sack of stones.

"Again?" Amihan Guinto looked worn out and disappointed as only a parent could. She grunted and stood up from the concave sofa. "Put him here. I'll take a look."

"How was your shift?" Marmeg asked as she helped Jeffy lie down. The metal frame creaked under his bulk.

"Miss Stevens missed the bedpan again so I guess it was a normal day," Amihan said. She rummaged through a kitchen cabinet. "Take that unnatural junk off, Mary Margaret."

Marmeg was tempted to refuse, but she needed to do a once-over on her gear anyway. She dropped the parts in a heap. Amihan walked by, carrying the odor of warmed-up chicken adobo and rice with her. Marmeg hadn't eaten since the afternoon, before her shift at the club. Her stomach rumbled as she helped herself to some leftovers while her mother patched up Jeffy's wounds.

Amihan hadn't objected when Marmeg learned to program. She'd expressed cautious optimism when Marmeg began winning contest money, but she had never approved of embeds or moots or any modern trend. *Elective surgery goes against God and the Pope.* Marmeg had heard the words often enough that they were tattooed on her brain.

Her mother had kicked her out after her first chip implant, but Marmeg could easily match her mother for stubbornness. She'd lived on the streets, spending the nights in homeless shelters when she couldn't crash with her friend T'shawn. Luck had landed her some workable exoskeleton discards and then the club security job. The money was enough to split rent with her mother, which let Amihan relent while saving face.

Marmeg washed her plate and then sat with her equipment. Her embedded control chips were legit, but the surgery to put them in wasn't, and her exoskeletal gear was filched from trash bins in rich neighborhoods. The pieces tended to break. She had backup parts to rube a fix during the race, but she'd rather catch a loose bolt or hairline crack now than in the mountains.

"Have you registered for the certificate program yet?" Amihan asked.

"Yes," Marmeg replied, staying focused on the pieces of gear scattered about. She'd filed the forms, not the payment.

"Did you get a spot in the elder care program?"

"Mm-hmm."

She had requested a spot, but she was stalling the registrar at UCLA with promises of tuition. As long as she placed in the top five in tomorrow's race, she'd have the money to start a four-year embed degree program. Real degrees led to real money, and that's what she needed to live on her terms, not her mother's.

"I know you're disappointed, mahal, but four-year colleges won't qualify a postnatal for financial aid. Working in the nursing home isn't that bad."

"No? Our life is so good?"

"There's food on the table," Amihan said sharply. "My children are healthy, except for this idiot." She nudged Jeffy.

"And all of us born unlicensed."

"So, we don't get free education and health care. You can't have everything handed to you on a gold plate. Let's be grateful for what God has given us."

"I am, Ma, but I want more. Six-digit ratings. Big money and benefits jobs. Make some rules, even with no vote. Run the world. Not be run down by it."

"Are you calling me run-down?"

Marmeg pressed her lips together. She had no safe answer to that question.

"Look at me! Four kids, and my body still looks great. My tits aren't saggy. My ass is nice. When I'm out after my shift, men buy me drinks."

"That explains the four kids," Marmeg muttered.

A slap against the back of her head knocked the multi-tool out of her hand.

"Hey! That's—"

"Don't disrespect your mother. My body only bears children when God wants, and I've been married every time."

"So, He doesn't give a shit if your kids are unhealthy, uneducated, under—"

This time, the blow landed hard across Marmeg's cheek, making her face burn and her eyes sting.

"Take that vile metal filth and get out! Go back to your club! Surround yourself with those people who deny God's gifts. Go! Ugly, ungrateful child."

Marmeg clamped down on the surge of answering violence. Even without the exoskeletal enhancements, her body was bigger and stronger than her mother's. Self-defense or not, if she hurt Amihan, she'd be the one feeling lower than a worm.

"Ma?" said a sleepy voice from the hallway. Then, "Marmeg!"

A small body clad in faded cupcake pajamas hurtled into Marmeg. She wrapped her little brother in her arms and glared over his shoulder at their mother. *Your yelling woke them up!*

"It's late, Felix. Go back to bed," Marmeg said.

The six-year-old was wide awake now, and he spotted Jeffy on the sofa.

"Again?" He almost sounded like their mother.

"He'll be fine," Marmeg and Amihan said simultaneously.

"Go to sleep, Felix, or you'll be feeling it on your backside."

Marmeg kissed the soft brown cheek and then stood, picking her little brother up in a smooth motion. "I'll tuck you in."

Lee was fast asleep on the upper bunk as Marmeg laid the baby of the family in the lower.

"Tell me a story?" Felix wheedled.

"Not tonight. It's late."

"You say that every time," he grumbled.

He had a point. Marmeg left anyway, knowing that Felix would draw her further into the argument if she stuck around. She glanced balefully at their mother. *That was your fault*, she wanted to say, but she kept the peace for the sake of her brothers.

"I'm tired," Amihan said, some of the shrillness gone from her voice. She walked toward the bedroom. "I'm going to bed too."

"Fine," Marmeg said.

She finished tuning up the exos and then pulled a large nylon backpack from the hall closet. She loaded it with spare parts and repair tools. A shabby plastic poncho went in too, in case the slight chance of rain materialized. The bag was old, with multiple patches of duct tape, but it held. She was about to put it on when Jeffy groaned from the sofa.

"Marm," he said, motioning her over.

She walked back and knelt by the sofa.

"You goin'? Tonight?"

"Yeah. Midnight bus to Fresno. Six o'clock to Oakhurst. Run or hitch from there. You be okay to watch the littles tomorrow?"

"Don't worry 'bout me. You focus on this race. You got 'nough money?"

As if her brother had any to spare. "Be okay, long as I place."

"An' if you don't?"

"But I will."

"That's my girl. You take care. An' kick some ass, eh?"

Marmeg smiled lopsidedly. "Hooah."

She tried to find a clean inch on her brother's face to kiss and settled for the top of his head. He was snoring by the time she reached the front door. A glance at her cuff told her that she couldn't catch the bus in time on foot.

She sent T'shawn a message: NEED A RIDE FROM HOME TO BUS CENTRAL. YOU FREE?

The response came a minute later. BE RIGHT THERE.

Ten minutes later, T'shawn pulled up in an old two-seater that he'd inherited from his uncle. The young man himself was tall, skinny, and garbed in his typical outfit of baggy jeans and a loose, long-sleeved shirt. His goggles—a relic from age twelve—were wrapped around his head. They were his first project. He'd fit the lenses from his regular glasses into old blue swim goggles that he'd found in the trash near school. When he showed up to classes wearing them, Marmeg was terrified for his safety, but he was so casual and confident that derision fell off him like paint flakes from his car. He did get beaten up later that day, but, as he'd pointed out to Marmeg when she patched him up, the goggles had saved him from yet another pair of broken glasses.

These days, T'shawn had such high black-market ratings that no one with a working brain would harass him. He still wore the goggles.

Marmeg smiled at him as they clasped arms, each one's hand to the other's elbow.

"What got you late?" he said.

The car's electric motor whined to life, and they pulled away from the curb.

"Jeffy had a 404."

"Gonna get himself killed one day. Can't be rescuing him always, Marm. You almost missed the bus."

"Know it, but he's my brother. Had my back all these years. Gotta look out."

T'shawn nodded, then shrugged. "Be growing up, getting yourself out. You win Sierra, he'll be on his own.

Oh, yeah, got some treats for you."

He took a small case from the car's center console and handed it to her. Four tiny capsules nestled in gray industrial foam. They gleamed with gold and green.

"New chips?"

T'shawn grinned. His teeth reflected white in the lights of opposing traffic, his face a dark shadow. "Payback for your latest code. Done my clients real good; said they did parkour times a hundred. Clean getaway last night."

"Don't tell me."

"Black market pays."

"Sure, but don't gotta like it. Want a better way."

"That's why you racing tomorrow. Don't be grumpy, Marm."

She smiled. Even if she didn't like his clients, she couldn't hold a grudge against T'shawn. Legit sales channels demanded certifications she couldn't afford. Yet. She closed the case and slipped it into her gear bag. The capsules were identical to the ones Marmeg had in her body. Those had also been rewards from T'shawn and his friends in dark places.

They arrived at the bus station ten minutes before midnight. Marmeg grabbed her bag and stepped out into a cloud of diesel fumes. She coughed and thanked her friend for the ride.

"Good luck," T'shawn said.

"Owe you for this, brud."

"It's nada. You go win."

The car behind them honked. T'shawn rolled his eyes, gave her a salute, and pulled away.

Marmeg walked into the squat concrete bus station. Security guards in bulky exos watched her motions as they did with anyone wearing gear. She found her bus and boarded it. The dozen other passengers were mostly migrant farm workers from Mexico and Southeast Asia. Half of them had already dozed off, and the others were staring at their screens.

Marmeg had a row to herself. Her pack sat next to her, bulky and comforting. She wrapped her arms around it and tried to sleep, to forget the flash of red after she'd paid for the one-way ticket to Oakhurst. Her account was zeroed.

~

The bus from Fresno to Oakhurst arrived late. Marmeg had intended to foot it from the small town to the starting line, but no way would she make it on time. She stood outside the station, staring at the distant peaks in despair. A woman emerged from the building and walked to her.

"I'm headed that way myself," the woman said. She

was obviously middle-aged and a nat, reminiscent of Marmeg's mother. "Want a lift?"

Thank God for the kindness of strangers.

Marmeg felt the first twinges of motion sickness as the pickup truck bounced and swayed through the curves of Sky Ranch Road. The woman—Lauren was her name—kept her eyes on the uneven dirt road, but she must have sensed Marmeg's discomfort.

"You want to turn back? It's not too late. You can still catch the bus to Fresno."

Marmeg explained, "Carsickness, not nerves." Then she shrugged. "Can't go back. Account's full busted. Gotta race. Gotta place."

"How old are you, sweetie? Does your mom or dad know you're up here doing this?"

"Twenty," Marmeg lied. "Mom knows."

They bounced through a particularly vicious dip. Marmeg's head smacked into the truck's ceiling on the rebound.

"Sorry," Lauren said.

Marmeg stared through the pockmarked but clean windshield. Trees towered above them on both sides. They mostly looked like elongated Christmas trees. Some had rusty red bark with a feathery texture. She was tempted to look them up on her cuff, but the thought of trying to read while her stomach lurched put her off.

Every few minutes, she caught a glimpse of rounded granite mounds: the peaks of the Sierra Nevada mountains.

"Here we are," Lauren said as she turned right into a large dirt clearing.

Dust rose around the truck as they pulled up next to the tree line. Sleek but rugged vehicles were parked nearby. The whole area swarmed with people.

Marmeg flicked her wrist to activate her cuff. The time read 8:35. She would not have made the nine o'clock cutoff on foot, not with all the enhancements in the world.

"Thanks," Marmeg said. "Owe you big. Credit you some grid time? Call it quits?"

Lauren raised her eyebrows. "What?"

Marmeg spoke in slower, fuller sentences. "Can't pay you back for the ride, but I got grid time to spare. Trade for your help. If you want."

"This was a favor, kid. You don't owe me anything. Just promise me that you'll make it through and back to your mom in one piece, okay? I've got a son not much younger than you. You remind me of him."

Marmeg ducked her head shyly.

"Deal. You look out tomorrow. See my name."

Marmeg ignored the bemused look Lauren gave her and hauled her bag out of the back. She waved once as

Lauren drove away. Dust stirred in the wake of the tires, making her sneeze. Its scent reminded her of the house-keeper who lived downstairs and always smelled of pine, though that was harsher than the natural version. Even the air smelled different from home—sharper, simpler.

Marmeg walked across the crowded dirt lot to the race booth. Journos surrounded former winners and high-rated contestants. Marmeg's heart beat faster. She was nobody today, but she knew that a few people had placed bets on her. Her odds were long—this was her first race—but they wouldn't be on her next one, not if she finished Minerva in the top five.

Contestants and their support teams clustered in small groups. Most had their screens out for last-minute tune-ups and optimized settings. A few were warming up. *Flashing their feathers,* Marmeg thought. She felt more than saw their curious glances as she walked by. Some-body snickered. Marmeg was glad of her brown skin. It hid the flush.

The registration booth was a modest structure made of canvas and plastic. A giant electronic panel across its top looked out of place as it displayed vid clips from previous Minerva Challenges. The corporate logo—a clock-work owl—hung on a banner to the left with the words EQUIPPING THE ATHLETES OF THE FUTURE printed below.

Two people sat behind the booth table. The one who faced outward was an attractive moot with short, floppy blond hair and a toothy smile. The other had zir back to Marmeg.

She dropped her gear bag on the dirt and waved her cuff over the screen on the table. It came to life and filled with upside-down text next to her picture.

"Mary Margaret Guinto?" the blond read.

Marmeg nodded.

Zie frowned. "Where's your support team? They need to check in too."

"My, uh, team?" Marmeg struggled to recall the race application and requirements. "They're late. Be here soon."

The other person behind the table turned around, and Marmeg startled at seeing zir—his—beard. She had assumed everyone here would be a moot.

"They need to meet you on the far side," he said, also frowning. He bent over the screen and flicked through Marmeg's registration. "You didn't put their names in the application. We'll need their information and your emergency contact's as well."

Marmeg scribbled three names with her index finger into the blank fields: Jefferson Marcos, Lee Inciong, Felix Inciong. Her brothers were the first people Marmeg could think of who didn't have a criminal record. Not that it would matter if the Minerva reps bothered to look them up—two of them were underage. She listed Amihan as her emergency contact.

Beard-guy rotated the display to face Marmeg. Tiny, dense text filled the page.

"Fingerprint at the bottom," he instructed.

Marmeg glanced over the section headers as she scrolled through pages of rules, regulations, waivers, and exclusions. She knew the rules well enough. The rest didn't matter. She pressed her thumb against the sensor. The blond grabbed Marmeg's other wrist, injected a subdermal chip, and slapped a Band-Aid over it.

"Race ID," zie explained. "Good luck, and see you on the other side."

Start time was in an hour. Marmeg found an unoccupied space near the trees to do a final gear check of her own. She examined the pins on the leg ports, making sure their alignment was good and the screws were tight. The torso shell came next. It made her feel like a turtle, but it was the best she had found in the castoff bin behind the used gear shop.

"What is zie wearing? Second generation exos?" said someone nearby.

"I think you mean *she*."

"Why are you picking on her, Zika?" asked a third, more melodious voice. "Worried about the competition?

She's brave to even go out in that kit."

Marmeg kept her body relaxed and ignored them. Doing security at the club had given her a fairly thick skin. She pulled muscle-enhancing sleeves over her arms and stuffed the skeletal-looking braces in the bag, hoping she wouldn't need to climb any overhangs. The braces only half-worked on the best of days. A quick systems check on her screen showed everything powered up and responding correctly.

An enormous tree trunk lay fallen at an angle a few yards away. Marmeg walked over to it. Its high point came up to her shoulders. She flexed her legs, crouched, and leapt to the top, landing lightly on the crumbling wood. A few heads turned to stare at her, and she quirked her lips. They wanted a show? Fine. She flipped backward off the tree, sprung off her hands, twisted midair, and landed on all fours.

Her audience shook their heads and returned to their tasks. Irked by the lukewarm reaction, Marmeg pulled her screen from the backpack and found the software she'd given T'shawn. *Parkour times a hundred*. She loaded the code into her chips.

She stood and flexed, testing the reaction time and spring coefficients. A mound of granite boulders the size of a small house was her target. She ran toward it. Cool alpine wind brushed her cheeks. Pine needles crackled underfoot. Crouch. Jump. Right foot on a near-vertical wall of rock. Push off. Land on the balls of the feet. Keep the momentum! Up, sideways with a hand and foot, diagonal. Pause.

She stopped for a few seconds at the highest point and chose her next target. She jumped, grabbed a branch, swung, flipped, and landed lightly enough to go straight into a run. Her breath came hard as she arrived at her gear bag. The air was sweet but thin. Marmeg didn't have the luxury of arriving a few nights early to let her body acclimate to the altitude.

"See that, Zika?" said the voice from earlier. "Maybe Cinderella will make it to the ball."

Marmeg almost laughed out loud. *My fairy godmother isn't done with her tricks.* She sipped at her water and then pulled up a motion analysis on her screen. A few tweaks to the rebound settings, and next time, she'd be able to run up the rock without using her hands.

Her cuff buzzed—two new messages and fifteen minutes to start time. Marmeg repacked her gear bag, cinching everything tight, and slung it over her shoulders as she walked to the trailhead. A cluster of people clad in smartskin and carrying next to nothing already stood there with distant gazes. Their lips moved and fingers twitched.

Someday, Marmeg promised herself, *I'll have all of*

that. Maybe even someday soon. She checked her messages.

WHERE ARE YOU? IF YOU'VE RUN AWAY FROM HOME, DON'T BOTHER COMING BACK: that was from her mother.

The second was T'shawn: GIVE ME YOUR GEAR IF YOU TOAST OUT?

OVER MY DEAD BODY, she sent back.

She ran a final download of map and satellite information before deactivating her grid access. That was the primary constraint of the Minerva Challenge. Stale data and live GPS would have to carry her through the race. The second requirement was to traverse a minimum of seventy-five miles before crossing the finish line on the eastern side of the Sierras. The record holder, from two years past, finished at a minute over eighteen hours.

The sun blazed through the heavy clouds for one eye-dazzling second, making Marmeg squint. When she looked around again, the crowd at the staging point had increased. A giant clock counted up to 10:00 AM on the screen above the registration booth.

"Double, double, toil and trouble," Marmeg muttered.

The person next to her, shiny from head to toe, smiled.

"What are you brewing?" zie said.

"Not me. Them." Marmeg inclined her head at the booth. "Stirring up some drama."

"I suppose they are. It's not like seconds or minutes matter at the finish. If they really wanted to make some excitement, they'd be funding Mountain Mike. So, is this your first race?"

"Yes. What's mountain mike?"

"Not what. Who," zie said, sounding amused. "He's a radical nat who lives in the backcountry. They always get a glimpse of him around the biggest accident sites, but they can't seem to catch him. You'd think it would be simple, him being a nat and all. Maybe living off-grid makes it easy to disappear."

Marmeg frowned. She hadn't planned for crazy forest nats.

"Don't look so worried," zie said with a laugh. "I think he's mostly a scare story. There are worse things for you to worry about. Like the rain. And have you deactivated your grid access? If it's on at the start, that's an instant disqualification. They're checking, you know?" Zie gestured at the camera drones buzzing overhead. "Those aren't all journos."

"It's off," Marmeg said.

Yes, her cuff showed that grid access was disabled. No more messages. No more support. She was on her own.

The clock display had switched to a countdown

timer. Ten seconds to go. Someone called a verbal version through the booth speakers. Drone-cams buzzed. Thunder rumbled in the distance.

"Good luck."

"You too."

"Zero!" boomed a voice.

The race opened like sand pushing through the neck of an hourglass. The lead contestants took off down the main trail at an easy run. Marmeg kept herself in their midst. A swarm of cameras flew above them, tracking every move and narrating the action to faraway viewers.

Being in the lead at the start had no correlation to being in the winners' list at the end, but it did boost your ratings. Most viewers only paid attention to the crowd during the open and the finish. The rest of the race belonged to the pros who could record and sell their whole experience as movies.

Marmeg pushed her body and her gear hard. A few heads turned in surprise as she passed them. Her breath came fast and shallow, but she gained until only three people remained ahead of her. If nothing else, she was in the top five at this moment.

They sprinted together over rocks and fallen trees. Dodged the grasping branches of low-growing bushes. Curved around trunks as wide as the pillars of City Hall. A cool wind brought the smell of rain.

The lead cluster spread out over the course of the first thirty minutes. People split off to follow their predetermined routes or took alternate ways around ponds and meadows. The other runners became blurs flitting between columnar trunks, far enough to be unobtrusive. The last drone camera had turned back at the twenty-minute mark, pushing the limits of its range.

Marmeg leapt on a fallen tree and used it to cross a boggy section. She skirted a car-sized knot of rotten wood at the far end and stopped to get her bearings. The other contestants had disappeared from sight. Like the fingers of a river delta, they would follow unique paths to the finish line. Her own route headed northeast toward the first of many low ridges.

As Marmeg ran, she heard nothing but the whispers of her footfalls and the wind through the trees. The rushing sound reminded her of rice pouring from a burlap sack. *Don't think about food,* she told herself. The clouds grew darker as she gained elevation. The air thinned and cooled. The light was dim for midday. Marmeg stopped to get a kinetic charger out of her gear bag and strap it to her left arm. Her cuff had solar cells, but they wouldn't be of much use in this weather.

She set her pace at a jog, leaping over the occasional fallen tree. Once, she startled a squirrel as she landed on the far side of a trunk. Had it been a snake, she could've been out of the race, like two years back when a contestant needed air rescue for a rattlesnake bite. She avoided blind jumps after that.

Heavy drops of rain spattered Marmeg as the trees dwindled. The pale hue of granite filled the widening gaps between reddish-brown trunks. In minutes, the woods went from sparse to nonexistent, replaced by boulders and twiggy bushes. A towering ridge rose from the open ground. Slabs of gray laced with pale blue and white loomed like sloppy icing on her mother's homemade cakes.

Marmeg grinned and raised her wrist to take a picture. Her brothers would be amazed that she'd climbed over this. Raindrops fell faster as she leapt from one mound to the next, the muscles of her legs reacting with unnatural force, driven by the exoskeleton. The journey to the top of the ridge was a dance. Jump. Twist. Take three delicately balanced steps to the left. Jump again.

A cramp in her right calf forced her to stop and adjust the exo's settings. Marmeg breathed heavily and took a break to look around from the high point. She stood on an island of stone surrounded by conical tips of dark green, a sea that undulated and shifted in color depending on the terrain. In the distance, sheets of rain obscured the serrated peaks that awaited her. Lightning flickered in her periphery.

She stared, unblinking, until she saw one strike in full. The jagged, white-hot flash was a phenomenon she'd never seen in her eighteen years of life in Los Angeles. Alone on the ridge, she thought to herself: *This must be how God felt after creating the world.*

A loud crack from behind brought her back to mortality. Lightning preferred to strike at exposed locations. She would be safer in the forest. Marmeg descended the ridge, favoring speed over grace. When she reached the shelter of trees, she slowed down. Rain trickled down her head in steady rivulets. The precipitation made a gentle rustle as it fell through the alpine canopy. The air had become noticeably cooler, and her wet state wasn't helping. Marmeg activated the heating coils in the torso shell.

Twenty minutes later, her breath came out in cottony white puffs, and she was colder than ever. She slipped a hand under the shell to confirm what she suspected: it hadn't warmed up.

Muttering curses in Tagalog that she'd learned from her mother, she stopped and reached into her pack. Her hand found the soft bundle of spare clothing.

Marmeg slipped out of the torso shell and sleeves. Goosebumps popped up along her bare arms. She pulled on a thermal shirt and a fleece sweatshirt with a faded US Army logo. Back on went the gear, and over that, the dollar-store plastic rain poncho. At least the torso shell's abdominal activators and cardio monitor still worked.

Some semblance of warmth returned after Marmeg jogged for a mile through the sodden trees. Her steps converged to an even rhythm. Her mind wandered to daydreams. She would finish her degree in embed design and get a "benefits job," as people said back home. If she was lucky, the company would pay for additional enhancements and surgeries. Then, once she was sufficiently buffed, she could quit and become a professional racer.

The pros had embedded audio and video recording capabilities with stereo sensors for immersive playback. The best had haptic sensors for whole-body virtual reality. Not many in the general public could use that level of technology, but the day was coming when they would. She had to become a star before that happened. That was the way out of the nat ghetto, to go from cash to credit to rich on ratings. This race was only the first step.

When she made it as a big-time embed racer, she could get her brothers in on the game. T'Shawn, too. They could be her legit support team. Maybe Felix would grow up to become an embed developer too. They could live in an actual house with separate bedrooms, and she would never have to share a bathroom again. Or worry about someone eating her food. She wouldn't even have to think about food, because she would hire someone to keep their fridge well stocked.

Best of all, if she were rich, she could have moot surgery and maybe convince her younger brothers to do the same. Jeffy was a lost cause, though he didn't hate moots like their mother did. And what would Amihan say about Marmeg's success? She would have to take back every nasty, negative comment she'd made about Marmeg's looks or smarts. She might even get licensed grandkids. Marmeg would gladly gift Jeffy the fees if he could stay with one girl long enough.

Her cuff beeped. She was off course by a quarter mile. She stopped running and traced a corrected path. Her sweat cooled. She shivered and looked up at the gray skies. They'd grown darker and more swollen with rain. *Keep moving, stay warm.*

She headed toward a mountain pass, the first of several on her planned route. The pass had looked smooth in the satellite images, an easy way to cross the first range. Maybe she'd meet another contestant there, though the pros preferred a challenge. Their sponsors paid for drama. This route did not promise excitement.

Marmeg was damp, chill, and borderline miserable when she arrived at the rock pile marking the climb to the pass. The rain had eased to a sprinkle. Cold had settled in its place like a determined, unwelcome houseguest.

Someone stood at the cairn. Marmeg was momentarily relieved at the sight of another human being, but she hung back, out of zir line of sight. Would this person be a friend or a foe? Given her mixed reception at the staging area, zie was as likely to scoff at or even sabotage her as zie was to be helpful. If only she could look up zir ratings on the grid, she would know the answer in seconds.

The person was staring at the space in front of zir face. Looking at maps, Marmeg assumed. She gathered her courage.

"Hoy," she called, coming forward.

Zie turned and focused on her. Zir eyes were almost black in the gloomy afternoon light. They were framed by long, curving lashes. This one definitely looked moot, with dark brown skin and curly black hair much like Marmeg's, though zie wore it to zir shoulders. It hung damp and limp in ropy waves. Zie had the slightest hint of curves at chest and hip, enough to be alluring but not enough to give away what zie was born with. Zie showed little sign of wetness and no signs of cold, wrapped as zie was in an expensive-looking smartskin.

"Hello. Are you headed up to the pass too?" Zie had an accent that Marmeg couldn't place.

"Firm."

"Pardon?"

"Yes. Up the pass."

"Great. We can walk up together if you don't mind the company."

Zie was rather cute. She wouldn't mind spending an hour with zir, and they'd have plenty of time to split up and get back to racing on the other side. *All or nothing,* she thought.

"Let's go."

They walked along something that resembled a path but was more of a clearing between scraggly bushes, boulders, and twisted trees. They made a course correction whenever one of them spotted the next stack of rocks that marked the way.

"My name is Ardhanara Jagadisha, but that seems to be a mouthful for Americans. You can call me Ardha."

"Arda," Marmeg repeated, trying to shape the unfamiliar sound.

"Close enough," zie said with a friendly smile. "So, what brings you to this contest?"

Chatty sort. Not her type after all.

"Prize money," Marmeg said.

Ardha let a few beats of silence pass. Zie must have been expecting more from her.

"I see. My father works for the Lucknow branch of Minerva, and the division there sponsored me to enter the contest. I'm mostly here to field-test their new technology, but the division wants publicity, too. If I win, they'll be able to push for an expansion of the design center there. I'm studying electrical engineering. I might even work there someday."

"Where's Lucknow?" Marmeg said, trying to keep up with zir words and strides. Ardha's smartskin was much lighter than Marmeg's old exoskeleton frames, and zie wasn't carrying a pack.

"India," Ardha said, sounding surprised. Zie waved at zirself. "You couldn't tell where I'm from?"

Marmeg shook her head.

"No tells on you. Full moot, full embed, right? It's good."

Ardha looked pleased.

"My grandparents are very progressive. They funded the sex surgery. For the embeds, I only had to pay for the implants. My sponsors donated the rest. So far, everything is holding up quite nicely. And your gear? Where is it from?"

Marmeg flushed as she thought about what to say. The truth wouldn't matter now, out here with no grid access and no way to update their ratings.

"Gear's filched, mostly," she confessed. "Got some legit chips—arms, legs, body." She tapped the base of her skull for the last one.

"What's 'filched'? I'm not familiar with that term."

"From a Dumpster. What some loaded embed threw

out."

"So, you picked up your gear from . . . a garbage bin?" Ardha's face wrinkled in repulsion and then smoothed into neutrality. "We're very careful to recycle all of our used gear so that it doesn't fall into criminal hands. Of course, there's so much corruption back home that the real criminals are running the country. That's a different problem. So, isn't this filched gear broken?"

"Fix it. Rube it." Marmeg shrugged. "Been doin' since I was eight."

Ardha's eyebrows shot up. "You've been repairing embed gear since you were eight years old? You must be very bright. How many sponsors do you have?"

"Nada."

Ardha turned and stared at Marmeg.

"Zero," she clarified.

"Yes, I understood that. I was simply speechless. Unusual for me, I know," zie said. "But how is this possible?"

"Born unlicensed. Bought my own later, but sponsors don't like that. Amnesty parents, kids—too much contro. Can't use us to sell their stuff."

"Ah, yes. I had forgotten about the new American caste system. If you're racing without any sponsorship, what will you do if you can't finish? There's a heavy fine for being extracted mid-race. You know that?"

Marmeg shrugged again.

Something small and white drifted by. Then another. And another.

"Snow?"

"So it seems. I didn't see that in the weather forecast. Did you?"

Marmeg shook her head.

"This should make the race more interesting."

Ardha reached back and pulled up a snug-fitting hood around zir head. Only zir face was exposed now. Tiny white flakes landed on zir brows and eyelashes, glittering there for a few seconds before melting away. Zir breath came in gentle puffs.

Marmeg, working much harder, exhaled clouds of white. She wished she had thought to pack a warm hat. It hadn't occurred to her that they would need winter weather gear in late spring, especially in California.

The snow smelled incredible, somewhere between iced vodka and fresh rain. Bare mountain rock surrounded them. They'd left the trees behind and below. Up here, the only colors were wet cement, gunmetal grays, and white. The clouds hung heavy and close. Wind batted down at them and tossed tiny snowflakes into demented, gravity-defying spirals.

Marmeg squinted, trying to see how much farther they had, but the slope and weather combined to make that a challenge. Ardha saw what she was doing and did the same.

"Oh, bloody hell," zie said.

"What?"

"You'll see in a minute. Come on."

Ardha must have enhanced zir distance vision. Zie broke into a run as the granite surface flattened into a gentle incline. Marmeg followed. They stopped abruptly just before the ground turned white. A field of ice stretched before them, all the way up to the top of the pass. Sheer vertical walls of stone rose up on either side. All Marmeg could see through the gap was sky.

"Can you believe it? A glacier! I studied the satellite images extensively. This pass was supposed to be completely clear." Zie kicked at the ice. "We'll have to go back and take a different route."

"Nah. Let's rube it," Marmeg said.

She sat and pulled out every metal item from her bag, spreading them on the ground until it looked like she was surrounded by shrapnel. Ardha stared as if she had lost her mind. Marmeg ignored zir and examined one item after another. Most were spare parts for her leg and arm exos—screws, pistons, actuators. The screws were too small, but the multi-tool with screwdrivers and blades? That had potential.

Marmeg showed Ardha the small device. "Cut this up. Strap on the sharp bits. Could get us over."

"Are you serious?"

"Yeah."

"You'd help me through the pass?"

"Sure. Splitsville after."

"That's . . . very sportsmanlike of you."

"Got a prob, though." Marmeg looked at the rest of the debris. "No metal cutters."

Ardha held out zir left hand as if zie wanted to shake. A sharp, two-inch-long blade pushed out of zir palm, just below zir pinky finger. Blood welled around the base of the blade, then congealed quickly into a brown scab.

"It will cut through metal like butter, or so they promised me. I didn't think I'd need it, but one of the engineers insisted. Give me the army knife."

Marmeg placed the multi-tool into Ardha's right hand and tried not to look envious. As the engineers had predicted, Arhda's blade sheared the hinge off with no effort. The various tools slid out and fell to the ground.

"Got a drill, too?"

"Yes. Right here in my index finger."

Ardha retracted the blade, and Marmeg watched in fascination as zir skin speed-healed over the wound. A small drill bit poked through zir right index finger. Marmeg pulled off her boots.

"Drill here and here," she said, pointing.

The drill made the barest whine as Ardha punctured

the reinforced carbon steel lining of her boots. Ardha's boots were much thinner, and zie put holes in them to match hers. While zie worked on zir boots, Marmeg attached the tools—one screwdriver tip and one short blade for each foot. It was a poor substitute for crampons, but their enhanced balance could make up for it.

"The pass must have been in shadow for the latest satellite images," Ardha grumbled as zie worked. "I don't see how else we could have missed the ice. Do you?"

Marmeg nodded. "Sure. Image hack. Get a high-rater to post it. Fooled us, yeah?"

Ardha frowned. "I hadn't thought of that."

Marmeg pulled on her boots. Her toes were stiff with cold, and she wiggled them against the interior to get back some warmth.

"I should have asked them to include a routine for walking on ice. If only we were allowed grid access, I could download one."

"Could code one."

"Here? Now? Write an ice-walking routine?"

Marmeg had her screen out and was scanning the subroutine that handled slip and balance. "Needs a few adjustments. Tweak the numbers in here. Might help." She blew on her fingers to warm them up and typed in an option to run with lower friction. If it didn't work, she'd need a quick way to return to her normal settings.

"Can I use your software?"

"What chips you got?"

Ardha didn't carry a screen—zie didn't need one—so Marmeg waited for zir to read her the information. The verdict was a no. Ardha's chips were a new design with a new instruction set. She didn't carry compilers for it.

"Sorry," she said, downloading the new routines into her legs. "You got a compiler?"

Zie shook zir head. "I don't even have source code. It was worth a try, though. I can't believe you can write code on the spot like this."

"Did contests in school. Gotta work fast."

Marmeg was happy to have come this far without having to fix any equipment. Her cuff showed three hours and eleven miles, well below the record-setting pace, but she wasn't after a record. Even fifth place awarded enough cash to buy one semester's tuition and Felix's license.

"Are you ready?" Ardha said, standing gracefully on zir cobbled boots and holding out a hand.

Marmeg quirked an eyebrow and pointedly ignored zir as she pulled on her pack. She crawled over to the ice field and cautiously stood. She slipped a bit with the first few steps. Then her gyros, chips, and brain figured out how to dance on ice.

Ardha was now holding out both zir arms as if to

catch her. It reminded her of a live ballet performance she'd seen years ago with her mother.

"Wanna dance?" she said with a wide grin.

Ardha laughed. "I'd rather race." Zie took off up the snowbound slope with rapid but choppy steps.

"Cheat!" Marmeg called after zir.

Then she tried leaping, inspired by the thought of ballerinas. She reached down mid-jump to one leg, then the other, increasing the spring tension. In less than a minute, she leapt past Ardha. The software routine worked beautifully.

Exhilaration soared when she arrived at the top. A glance back showed Ardha jumping but also slipping and counterbalancing as zir smartskin failed to accommodate for rubed crampons. Zir face was drawn with concentration, eyes scanning the ice for the best course.

From the peak of the pass, Marmeg caught her first view of the vastness ahead. Waves upon waves of sharp, rocky peaks continued out to the horizon. Many were shrouded in clouds, and the valley itself was obscured by the haze of falling snow and rain. Somewhere, on the far side of it all, lay the striated columns of Devils Postpile and the finish line.

Ardha stopped next to her, admiration clear on zir face. "Thank you for the assistance. That saved me at least thirty minutes of rerouting." Zie reached down and snapped off the blades from zir boots.

"Keep them."

"I would, but I have no pockets."

They both laughed. It was true: zir smartskin was smooth and almost featureless. Marmeg took the blades back, snapped off her own, and stowed them in her pack. When she straightened, Ardha wrapped her in a brief but gentle hug. Her friend—because it seemed that's what they were now—had a warm, smooth cheek that smelled subtly of roses.

"See you on the other side. Good luck!"

"Luck," Marmeg replied.

The embrace had startled her, but she didn't mind it. As Ardha pulled away, Marmeg caught a flicker of motion in the corner of her eye.

"Did you see—" she said, but zie was already running down the slope.

Marmeg looked around but didn't see any signs of life. Odd, she thought. Perhaps an animal, though anything big that was up this high was not something she wanted a good look at. She recalled the story about Mountain Mike. A tingle of fear ran through her. Then a sudden gust of wind almost knocked her over and loosed the feeling from her head.

There was no one there but her, and she had to move. Marmeg flicked her wrist and pulled up the route map on her cuff. It headed in a different direction from the way Ardha had run. Zir silver form shrank in the distance. *Good.* She didn't want to spend too much time getting friendly with the competition.

～

The weather worsened as Marmeg traversed the undulating wilderness. Down she went into the quiet of trees, green and gloom, damp earth and soggy pine needles. Up, through scrub and rock, over a small rise with a local view. Down again. Her steps treacherous as ice crystallized in the shade. She climbed and descended until the repetition became mind-numbing.

Three hours and thirteen miles passed by with no company but an occasional squirrel dashing for shelter. Once in a while, Marmeg heard a rustling sound—usually when she'd stopped to catch her breath or tweak her leg settings—but she never spotted the source of the noise. Deer? Bear? She didn't have any weapon but the broken multi-tool blades, and those would offer poor protection against an angry or hungry animal. Better that the creature stayed hidden.

She was leaping cautiously up a rock-strewn ridge, now speckled with patches of invisible ice, when her right arm froze in mid-swing. That threw off her already delicate balance. She came crashing down into a nearby bush.

Marmeg winced as she tried to stand. Her left hip was bruised, and her arm was locked into a right angle. She got up awkwardly and walked to a sheltered rock under a tree. Using her working arm, she tried to pull off the right sleeve. It was completely rigid. She took her screen out of the pack, unrolled it, and pulled up the diagnostic software.

A quick check of the sleeve showed everything reading normal. With a grimace of annoyance, Marmeg called up its controller chip next. Every register read back an ominous set of zeroes. She tried sending the reset code, but it made no difference. Either the chip or its communications was fried.

Marmeg looked up into the feathery dark-green needles and let out a stream of curse words that she'd learned from one of her stepfathers. Now what? She could try to keep running with a locked arm. She could cut the damn sleeve off, though it would be worthless forever after. Or she could give up, turn on her grid access, and quit.

The third option wasn't a real choice. Not yet, though the likelihood of her placing in the top five was looking a lot lower than it had ten minutes before. Fixing the sleeve would take too much time, but she might as well preserve it as long as possible.

Her hip throbbed, probably from landing on a rock. Her right shoulder ached from the weight of the frozen arm. She chose the first option.

Marmeg grabbed the stim pills out of the backpack and downed two. Then she pulled out an old leg sleeve that she'd brought as backup gear and used it to make a sling. She shivered as she stood. The cold had seeped in quickly while she sat still. She headed onward in a slow jog, wary of every obstacle.

~

An hour later, the weather went from bad to worse as rain turned to sleet and intermittent hail. Marmeg's plastic hood grew heavy with ice crystals. Her leg motions became sluggish. The temperature must have dropped low enough to thicken the hydraulic fluid.

She was halfway across a fallen tree over a raging stream when the leg exos stopped working. Marmeg was stuck like a horse rider in a glitched fantasy game, both legs completely immobile. She tried to warm up the pistons with her mobile hand, but that had no effect.

No way could she remove her exoskeletons while perched ten feet above frigid, frothing water. Instead she scooted, a painstaking few inches at a time, until she was on the other side. There, she swung one leg over the top and landed on her knees in a soggy clump of ferns.

"Are you testing me?" Marmeg said out loud.

Her mother's God might or might not have been listening, but she was tired of being alone. And just plain tired. The cuff showed the time as five-thirty and her mileage at twenty-nine—less than four miles per hour and well under the four-point-two record, but not bad, either. Where was everyone else, she wondered, and how were they faring in this weather?

The background image on her cuff switched to a picture of her brothers. Seeing their faces made tears sting the backs of her eyes.

"Want to go home," she whispered to the cuff.

Off-grid as she was, nobody would be listening.

"I'm cold. One of my chips is fried. Ice is falling from the sky. Forecast said rain. This isn't rain! Okay, God? You got that? Want me to fail? Teaching me a lesson, like Ma always said you would? Well, screw you! I'm not a quitter."

The words were a small comfort against the constant patter and crunch of frozen droplets making their way through the trees. Marmeg repeated the last few words like a chant while unscrewing and removing the leg braces. After they were off, it occurred to her to check the embedded chips in her legs.

All four were toast.

Marmeg's scream ripped through the silence and faded into the gentle chatter of precipitation. She kicked viciously at one of the exos. It flew into the muddy, half-frozen stream bank. Her mind reeled. How could five of her embedded chips choose this day, this race, to stop working?

Virus, whispered a voice in the back of her brain.

The chips had programmable boot codes, ones that Marmeg could access using the near-field emitter from her screen. The last time she'd been up close with other people was back at the race start. Someone must have planted the virus with a built-in delay, like a ticking time bomb.

She tested the core chip, the one lodged in her brain stem, and almost cried with relief when it responded correctly. She wiped its memory and reloaded clean code from her screen. That one, at least, wouldn't fall victim to the virus. She did the same for her left arm.

What next? The sun wouldn't set for three hours, but it was getting close to the mountain peaks in the west. The sky was dark with clouds, and the air wasn't getting any warmer. She was facing down a long, cold night with ordinary legs, no heat, and no shelter.

Bail out, she thought. *It's over. You can't win this. You'll be lucky not to freeze to death.*

Then she remembered the spare chips, the last-minute gift from T'shawn, that she'd tucked into her gear bag.

"Crazy talk," Marmeg whispered.

But her left hand moved, took the small blade from the broken-up multi-tool, sliced through the right sleeve. She wouldn't attempt surgery with only one arm. With both arms free and mobile, she rummaged inside the pack until she found the box.

Four clear capsules nestled in dark gray foam. Inside them, tiny wafers of silicon and gold gleamed in the half-light of late afternoon. Delicate threads of wire lay coiled beside each capsule, the ends surrounded by a protective sheath.

Marmeg had been awake for the original surgeries. T'shawn had held her hand. They'd watched in fascina-tion as Marmeg's leg was numbed; as the surgeon sliced into the flesh of her calf; as he pulled up a quarter-inch flap of bloody skin and muscle. Then he'd tucked a cap-sule into the incision, threading the lead wires into the muscle fibers, and stitched it up neatly.

Marmeg rolled up one pant leg and traced the old scar with an icy finger. The stim pills ran through her veins, but they wouldn't help much with this. She gritted her teeth, took a deep breath, and pushed the short, dull knife into the scar.

An agonized groan turned into a sob. Blood welled

and fell onto the spring green leaves of the fern below like crimson rain. With a trembling hand, Marmeg reached into the cut. She whimpered as she felt for the capsule. When she touched something hard and slippery, she grabbed and yanked. The leads pulled free of the muscle. Adrenaline and endorphins surged. Her heart raced.

The sudden wrench of her stomach caught Marmeg by surprise. She bent over to the side and managed not to throw up on herself. Then, taking a few shaky breaths, she carefully removed a new capsule, unwound the leads, and pushed it into her leg. She shoved the leads apart as best as she could, and then stopped. There was nothing to suture with, not that she even knew how.

Frustration and despair took over like fog filling a valley. Her heart hammered. *Think, you stupid, lousy brain! You wanted to do this race. You thought you could take these people, but you're useless! Just another crapshoot filcher who doesn't know a damn thing about being an embed.*

Glue.

She had glue in the pack.

Marmeg found the small tube of industrial-strength fixative. *Don't glue your fingers to your leg.* She sobbed and laughed. She stanched as much blood as she could with the ruined sleeve and then squeezed glue along the outer part of the incision. She pressed down with one hand while wrapping the useless, ripped fabric around her leg like a bandage. With a shaky sigh of disbelief, she sat back and stared at her handiwork.

"Not bad, but what'll you use to tie off the other three?" a deep voice said from behind.

Marmeg screamed, leapt up, and then cried out from the pain in her calf. In the shadows of the trees stood a tall, wiry man with a face from a nightmare: dark, dirt-streaked skin, wild hair to his shoulders, features hidden behind a coarse beard. Marmeg's tiny blade was lying on the ground. It might as well have been on the moon.

"What—who are you?"

"Let's save the introductions for later. Right now, we need to get you warm and clean that wound up before you contract a raging infection."

The words took a minute to penetrate the fear pounding through her head.

"Why?"

He raised a bristly eyebrow. "Why what?"

"Why help me?"

"Don't trust me, eh? Well, that's not a bad instinct for a kid like you in a place like this. Too bad you didn't think of it earlier when you were with the other racer. Now come on. Save your questions for when we're inside. I swear I'm not going to hurt you."

The man grabbed Marmeg's muddy exos and the rest of her gear, including the bloodied blade, and shoved it all into her pack. He pulled the bag onto his back with a grunt.

"What the hell is in here? Weighs as much as a small person."

"Gear."

He snorted, then tried to put an arm around Marmeg. She instinctively twisted away and shoved, but she was the one who lost her balance and fell on the ground. He looked at her with a bemused expression.

"Fine. You go ahead and walk on your own."

He moved away, threading a path between the plants and trees. Marmeg limped after him.

$\sim$

A short but painful walk brought them to a log cabin. The low building nestled under the trees next to a lush, green meadow. The mountain man pushed open a wooden door. Marmeg followed him into a one-room cabin. A cot, a table, and a tree stump stool made up the furnishings. A locked metal chest was tucked under the table. Across from the door, in the corner, stood an oblong black thing, about the size of a large pot, with a metal tube leading out of it and through the roof. Dim light filtered in through a dirty window.

The man busied himself with the black device, pushing small pieces of wood in through a door in its front. Then he grabbed a box, took out a toothpick-looking thing, and struck it against the side. The toothpick lit up, and he tossed it in with the wood. As Marmeg watched in fascination, the smaller pieces caught fire, and soon everything started to burn.

The man noticed her fixed gaze. "It's a wood-burning stove."

"Not legit."

"That's true. It's illegal in California to burn anything that smokes, but it's the only way to survive out here."

"You Mountain Mike?"

His eyes twinkled. "Is that what they're calling us?"

Marmeg caught the plural. "Who else?"

"We're a network. Now, enough standing around. You'd better lie on the bed while I look at that hack job you did on your leg."

The stove warmed the cabin. Marmeg sank onto the cot, wary but glad of the comfort. The mattress had lumps and smelled moldy, but it was better than a bed of pine needles. Pain wrenched at her leg as she swung it onto the pallet.

Mike, or whoever he was, had removed a plastic box with basic medical supplies from the metal trunk. He placed the stool next to the bed, sat, and cut away her makeshift bandage. His face twisted into a grimace as he examined the wound.

"I can't do much, but I'll disinfect the outside and cover it with sterile gauze. You'll have to get it looked at tomorrow after you're back in civilization. What I can do," he said, glancing briefly at her before looking back at the leg, "is help you with the other calf chip. I've got rubbing alcohol to clean off that knife blade some, and I can make a better incision than you can. Will you let me?"

Marmeg winced as he applied the ointment. If he'd wanted to hurt her or kill her, he could've done so by now, and she could use the help. Then again, nothing in life was free.

"Why? What you want of me?"

"Your word that when you win this race, you'll help our movement."

"Help how?"

"You give us half your prize money."

"Half! If I don't?"

"We'll provide evidence to Minerva of this encounter—that you took help from me—and they'll disqualify you and take their money back."

"If I don't place?"

"You will. You might even come in first. The people we help always end up in the top three."

Marmeg frowned. "All cheats? Every year?"

"The last four years. That's when we first got the idea.

I suppose it's cheating, but it's a win-win situation the way I see it. We choose someone who deserves a little help, like you, and we get to keep doing our work."

That explained the dark horse winners.

"Look around, kid! Nature isn't static, and it's always full of surprises. Take this cold front right now. Everyone comes into these races believing they just have to be strong and fast, that studying images of the terrain and digital maps is enough to know what they're going to get. It rarely is. You know that already from that glacier you and the other fellow had to climb."

"You were there? Thought I saw someone."

Mike nodded. "You did, but it wasn't me. We've been watching from the start. That's how we know who to pick. We have to be careful, choose someone who could plausibly win. Now let's get back to the question at hand: do you want my help with that other calf? Do you want to win this race?"

Marmeg looked down at her cuff and her brothers' goofy smiles. She didn't have to tell them the whole story, but she did have to come home with some money. It was that or call her mother to come bail her out. That was the worst possibility Marmeg could imagine.

Amihan would never forgive Marmeg for the enormous sin of spending her money on gear and race fees. She would call it gambling. And she would be convinced that God was punishing Marmeg for partaking of such an evil pastime. She might be right, considering that Marmeg would be back to club security and nothing more if she didn't place. Winning by any means, even for half the prize money, would be better than that.

"Do it."

Mike handed her a few white pills. "These won't help with the pain now, but they will later."

He went back to the trunk and pulled out a dark-brown glass bottle. He worked the cork out and handed Marmeg the bottle. She washed the pills down in one swallow, glad that Jeffy had given her opportunities to drink cheap booze. At least she didn't make a fool of herself by choking on whatever this was. It burned the back of her throat. A pleasant, tingling warmth soon spread through her body. She leaned her head back against the rough wood and closed her eyes.

"You go ahead and scream if you need to. Nobody's around to hear it."

That sounded like a line in a bad horror vid. Marmeg chuckled, but she kept her eyes closed. The sounds of gear clinking played counterpoint to the pops and crackles from the wood stove. The scent of smoke filled the air. Marmeg sank into a stupor.

A sensation of cold and wet against her leg snapped her eyes open. Mike rubbed an alcohol pad against the old incision on her other calf.

"Ready?" he asked.

"As ever."

Marmeg lay on her side and clenched her hands around the edge of the mattress. Mike sliced into her flesh, a quick, sure cut. She gritted her teeth against the pain; no screaming, not this time. She was breathing fast and harsh by the time he dug in with a pair of tweezers and extracted the bad chip. While he disinfected the replacement, she took a deep, steadying breath and reached for the brown glass bottle. She gulped three times.

"You better put that down before I finish this."

He was much more deft with the capsule placement than she had been. She was surprised that he knew what to do. Unlike her field surgery, he took the time to close the wound neatly, wiping it clean before applying the glue. The result was a red, ragged mess, but it looked better than her other leg.

"I'm not going near the quad chips and your femoral artery." He handed Marmeg her screen. "Your turn."

She pulled up the control software and reprogrammed the new capsules. She had splurged for a brainstem chip as her only legit surgery, using the programming contest money she had ferreted away from her mother. One of its benefits was that her muscles adapted more quickly to program changes. Another was that new chips would integrate faster with her physiology. The pain, however, was something she would have to ignore for the next twelve hours.

Marmeg hissed as she limped to the table where her gear pack lay open. She gritted her teeth, pulled the calf exos on, and went through a basic test sequence: walk, run in place, jump, balance on one foot. The incisions twinged but the pain intensity decreased with every flexion and extension of her muscles.

As a final exercise, Marmeg jumped from the floor onto the table, landing on it in a crouch and poised for her next motion. Mountain Mike leaned against the door, his arms crossed across his narrow chest, his expression inscrutable under the facial hair. His eyes followed her movements.

Marmeg leapt lightly off the table and repacked. She left the two quadriceps exos out. They wouldn't be worth much on the open market. She'd have plenty of time to replace them once she was done with this race, though she wouldn't have much money, not after she shared with the Mikes. That meant no license for Felix.

"What'll you do with your half?" she said, stowing the last of the gear.

"We use it to keep up the knowledge of how to live with the land. When catastrophe strikes, which it inevitably will, what are you embeds going to do? Your gear makes you dependent on technology. Same with everyone who never leaves the city. Without electricity and clean water and food delivered to you, you'll be lost. You'll need people like us to show you how to survive. Someone has to keep the old skills alive."

Mike was busy at the stove, poking inside with a metal rod and splashing water into it from a bucket that Marmeg hadn't noticed before. The flames died down into glowing bits of wood and burnt black sections. He closed the stove door.

"We also use the money to maintain these cabins, pay for our phones, and supplement our food. This land can provide a lot, but we get hungry for cake and beer sometimes, too." He grinned. His teeth were yellow but straight. "Let's go."

Marmeg followed him out of the cabin. Cold air struck her bare face. The sun had passed behind the western peaks, and icy rain had turned into flakes of snow. Marmeg's breath puffed out like a friendly ghost. She flicked on her cuff and checked their path. It wasn't taking them back to her original route.

"Where we heading?"

"Didn't you wonder how a bunch of survivalists like us could help you embeds win a race?"

"Wondered, yeah."

"We've made tunnels under the ridges and built

shortcuts through some of the passes as well. They're hidden from the satellites by plant cover. Nature does most of the work for us."

Marmeg's conscience pricked her. Cheats were not looked on favorably in her neighborhood, and Jeffy was especially contemptuous of people who didn't play fair. She hated the idea of lying to him. He'd supported her when she started fixing up embed gear. He'd slipped her money, shielded her from their mother's ire. Without him, she wouldn't be at this race today. She didn't want to let him down, but if she didn't place somewhere in the top five, she would disappoint everyone, especially herself.

Far behind them, thunder rumbled. They climbed up through the trees. The wind blew harder as the vegetation thinned out.

"I'm going to give you a new route," Mike said.

He stopped at the base of a large slab of rock that rose like a wall. Marmeg craned her neck, following the vertical expanse until it vanished into the clouds. A snowflake landed in her slack-jawed mouth, a tiny crystal of cold that dissolved on her hot tongue.

Mike pulled an old-style handheld from his back pocket. Marmeg flicked on her cuff and allowed him to send her a file. It was a map overlay, much like the one she had made, but with a far more direct route.

"'Nuf miles?"

"It'll be enough. Just don't hug the next racer you come across."

"What?"

"That boy you helped over the ice field. I'm fairly certain he's the one who fried your chips. It was probably when you let him get close."

"Zir," Marmeg corrected automatically while her mind raced. Had Ardha been close enough to corrupt her chips? Yes: that final embrace. But zie had been so co-operative. *Stupid, stupid, stupid!* To fall for a pretty moot face and destroy her chance of winning this race fair and square. She wished she could smash Ardha's rating then and there, make sure no one trusted zir again.

Mike shrugged. "Zie, he, she—until you change your genetics, you're still male or female as far as I'm concerned. You kids want to play at being something that you're not, that's between you. I'm not changing the way I talk."

"Not playing," Marmeg said irritably. "Making waves. Changing the world. Better to judge on what you can do, not how you born. Bodies are going out. Nats be left behind."

"You think so, eh? What do you expect will happen to the human species if we're all neutered embeds? Who's going to make the babies?" Mike shook his head. "You think you're going to change the world. The reality is that the world is changing us. Pretty soon we're going to need all the *nat* skills and abilities that our ancestors had. I should know; I used to be like you, full of bits of silicon and titanium. I fought in the Congo. Nature is stronger than we give her credit for. Best that we learn to coexist peacefully with her."

Not only was Mike a nat, he was a converted one—the worst kind when it came to preaching—but his words didn't convince her. Companies like Minerva specialized in physical enhancements, but others were working on deeper changes. They wouldn't need babies in the future. They would live forever, bodies enhanced, minds uploaded.

Mike looked at her and sighed. "Every year I try, hoping that the message gets through to someone . . . someday. You think you understand the world by seeing it through the grid, but reality is messier than bits and bytes."

They'd been walking along the base of the massive rock wall. Mike stopped at a cluster of scraggly bushes growing between some rocks. He pushed the branches aside and rolled a couple stones away, revealing an opening that was half Marmeg's height and as wide as an arm span.

"You'll see for yourself when you're older. Here's the

tunnel. Someone will meet you when you need to get into the next one."

"This? Be a tunnel?"

Mike grinned. "I never said you could run it. Trust me, you'll crawl through just fine. In fact, your calves are going to thank you while you're on your knees. It's too bad you lost the upper leg enhancements, but this will still save you a lot of time."

He took something out of his pocket and then stretched it over Marmeg's head.

"It's a head lamp. The switch is here, on top. Good luck. I'm going to cover the entrance once you're in, so don't try to turn back."

Marmeg looked at him like he was crazy, which he was, and then decided that she was equally crazy to do this. She got down on hands and knees, turned on the lamp, and went in.

~

The crawl went on and on until Marmeg's arms, legs, and back ached. She felt like it lasted for hours, but according to her cuff, it only took forty-five minutes. The sky was nearly dark by the time she emerged into another cluster of bushes and rocks.

She looked around but saw no one. She pushed rocks

across the hole and tried to arrange the bushes to hide it from a casual glance. The task was harder than it looked. After three attempts to make it seem natural, Marmeg shrugged and gave up. Let the Mountain Mikes make it better if they wanted to.

She loaded the map from Mike, oriented herself, and walked in the direction it indicated. As she moved, the kinks in her body relaxed into a minor nuisance. She tried jogging and then running. Jumping didn't work as well as it had with the quad exos, but at least the pain from her cuts faded to a dull ache. She could maintain a respectable pace.

Snow dusted the ground like powdered sugar on cinnamon cake. Marmeg's stomach growled. Her throat felt parched. The booze back at the cabin couldn't have helped with hydration. She opened her mouth and caught a few snowflakes on her tongue. They melted with a sensation like popping bubbles.

A laugh burst from her. She wished Felix were there. Lee and Jeffy, too. None of them had left the city, seen true wilderness. Here, with nothing but trees and snow, sky above, dirt below, Marmeg's spirit soared with glee. It had all gone to shit without a pot, but she was *there*. She was experiencing something that none of her family could comprehend, surrounded as they were by cement and glass.

Marmeg ran faster, breathing hard and enjoying the burn of cold air in her lungs. The incisions on her calves tugged with each step, but the sensation was gentle and far removed. Snow blurred into an almost uniform whiteness. She had to land each step by feel and hope her balance held. A trickle of sweat traced the space between her shoulder blades. Fingers and toes warmed as her blood pulsed and breath deepened.

"I'm alive!" Marmeg yelled into the dark expanse above.

She'd left the head lamp on. She slowed to a jog and switched it off, then activated the night vision in her contact lenses. Marmeg ran until she saw another massive slab of granite looming ahead. The time on her cuff showed nearly ten o'clock. She'd been out for eleven hours.

Her mileage showed as forty-five, far more than she expected. GPS access had been blocked inside the tunnel, so the routing software that Minerva required had extrapolated from the terrain. It calculated the miles as if she'd climbed over rather than crawled through. How had the Mountain Mikes found that loophole?

She arrived near the base of the mountain and couldn't go farther. The map indicated that she should turn left. Five minutes later, a figure loomed out of the darkness, its hooded face wrapped in a giant wooly scarf.

"This way," rumbled a low, decidedly male voice.

Marmeg looked for a beard, but it was impossible to find in the swaddled head, especially with her night vision on. The Mike said nothing more as he revealed the tunnel. He stayed silent even after she went in.

The light from the head lamp blinded her when she turned it on. Marmeg blinked and squinted until her pupils adjusted, then began the long, painful crawl to the other side. Muscles cooled, breath slowed, and a deep cold seeped into her body from the rock surrounding her.

This tunnel was considerably longer than the previous one and had some uphill and downhill sections. Halfway through an incline, the pain pills began to wear off. She couldn't get into the pack for more, so she gritted her teeth and kept moving. Her calves were screaming with pain by the time she came out of the other end. It was nearly midnight. All of the elation from earlier had evaporated.

Marmeg stopped to stretch her pain-wracked body. She popped a couple more stims and three pain pills into her mouth and tried to work up some spit. The mass went down in a painful, bitter lump that made her gag. The analgesics would take some time to work, but the stimulants were fast.

She sat and waited for them to hit. She hated this race. Winning by any means, cheating the GPS system, getting help—and for what? So she could give half the prize money to a group of people whose values meant nothing to her. This race was supposed to be her chance to prove herself, to prove that she could compete with those who had the latest and greatest tech. Now she was like every other lowlife filcher. She ignored the rules, broke laws, and stomped on anyone who stood in her way.

She checked her cuff. The mileage had jumped by another fifteen. That put her total at sixty miles with only fifteen more to go. If all her gear still worked, she could match her earlier four-miles-per-hour pace. She could finish the race and beat the record. Unless that, too, was faked.

Marmeg groaned and hit the ground with a fist. The faces of her brothers stared at her from the cuff.

"What should I do, Jeffy?"

The image was still, silent, accusatory.

You started this, it seemed to say. *Finish it! Don't be a whiny little girl. You've already done enough to be disqualified. You might as well go for the kill.*

Marmeg shuddered with cold. Too much time sitting still. Her calves stung at the incisions. She could feel warm blood as it seeped through the bandages and froze against the frigid air. Would bloody ice crystals look like rubies?

Red gems dripped from her legs and fell to the

ground, forming a carpet around her. The crystals caught the starlight, sparked with their own internal fire. A thousand tiny flames surrounded Marmeg with their warmth.

She woke with a start. The forest was black. Nothing but chilled dirt and melting snow lay beneath her.

"Wake up," she told herself, slapping her cheeks.

Her cuff said she'd been asleep for twenty minutes, and her body felt heavy from the weight of it. The stim pills had begun their work, though. With a soft groan, Marmeg stood and forced herself to walk, step by slow, dull step.

A quick check showed the leg exos and one remaining sleeve functioning correctly. The heating elements on the torso shell remained broken—no surprise—but the heart and lung monitors read correctly, and the abdominal boosters were doing their job. So, why couldn't she move faster?

You're tired.

She put one foot in front of the next, following the path set out for her. What else could she do? Around one o'clock, the moon rose above the eastern peaks. Its light showed breaks in the cloud cover. Marmeg couldn't see the stars she'd hoped for, but the moonbeams made for better company than the storm-clouded blackness. The snow had stopped falling. The ground crunched under her steps and glimmered from the faint light.

The pain pills started kicking in, and Marmeg picked up her pace. No matter what prize money she won, she wouldn't be out for another solitary moonlit hike any time soon. She'd caught a snowflake on her tongue. She'd heard ice crackle under her boots, mimicking the sound of broken glass that had been stepped on too many times. Or the sound facial bones made when your mom's boyfriend didn't much like your mom's kid.

She wished she could have a do-over, a second chance to prove that she was as good as the legit embeds and moots; that she could beat them at their own game; that she deserved to be at a university with people who were born licensed, who never had to worry about food or medicine or shots. But that kind of thinking trapped her in the dark corners of her mind, where bad ideas looped infinitely.

Maybe Mountain Mike was right. Life was never fair. Winning by cheating was okay if you used the money for the right reasons. In her case, she wanted to buy little Felix's license so he could get his shots and go to school. She wanted a full degree, which ultimately meant a better life for her and her family. Those goals were noble enough to let the ends justify the means, weren't they?

A figure loomed up out of the darkness. Marmeg gasped and nearly lost her footing. She stumbled to a halt a few feet away, breathing hard. When she looked at the person, she saw a face hidden under bushy hair that glinted in the moonlight.

"The hell?" Marmeg demanded, heart hammering. "No tunnels for miles yet!"

"You're this girl? The one with the leg cuts and all?" The muffled voice was high-pitched.

Marmeg peered at the Mountain Mike. "You a lady?"

The bundle of hair nodded. "We wear beards to fool the cameras. As long as we don't come too far into the open, they can't tell us apart. Follow me."

"But—"

"Come on!"

Marmeg bit back an irritated reply. This Mike plowed straight through the underbrush. Marmeg followed, small branches smacking into the backs of her calves and making the incisions sting. Her cuff said she'd been on the correct path to the next tunnel. Now they headed toward an overland route that she'd considered before the race. It was direct, but it required rock climbing skills and equipment that she didn't have.

They arrived at a tumble of boulders. Mountain Mike scrambled up on her hands and knees. Marmeg decided that she might as well take it easy and use all four limbs too. There wasn't much point in jumping like a goat when she had no idea where to go. What would they put her through next?

A light breeze blew over them and grew stronger as they climbed higher. Broken clouds outlined by ghostly white moonlight hung behind the ridge's saw-toothed silhouette. As she and Mike neared the top, the wind blew so hard that they were forced to lean into it. The bare rock was mostly free of snow and ice, though a few wind-sheltered pockets glittered like treasure. She scooped a handful into her mouth. Only a few drops of cold liquid, but the relief to her throat was immeasurable.

Mountain Mike tapped her on the shoulder and then pointed down—into the wind and a steep, rocky slope. She put her bristly face next to Marmeg's ear, and Marmeg fought the urge to pull away.

"There's someone down there who's hurt. Another contestant. I think you might be able to help me with him. Follow me very carefully. He went down this scree and got trapped under a rockfall. I don't want the same thing to happen to us."

Marmeg peered down, trying to see the other person. The nearer rocks reflected the moon's glow, but nothing else was visible. Her attention locked onto her footing once they transitioned to the down slope. Stones littered the ground, ranging in size from pebbles to boulders wider than her arm span. Each step sent a few of them skittering away. The rattle reminded her of gunfire, a sound that accompanied many nights at home.

Mountain Mike was doing a respectable job of the climb, though she ended up on her ass after half of her steps. Marmeg managed to keep her balance. The lack of full leg exos made the job more difficult than it should have been. She wondered how another race contestant had screwed this up.

Then she saw the massive vertical scar of pale gray against darker rock. At its base lay a jumble of boulders, and under that, the lower half of a body. She winced and turned away for a second, imagining what it must feel like to be crushed beneath that kind of weight. Her legs would be pulp.

Marmeg and Mike inched sideways, perpendicular to the slope, until they stood near the injured contestant. One look at the pale, unconscious face and Marmeg identified zir as Ardha. *You got what you deserved,* said the vengeful part of Marmeg's mind. *Shut up. Nobody deserves this*, said another.

Marmeg bent to lift a rock from Ardha's body.

"No!" Mike said. "Don't touch those rocks! I don't know how stable they are, and they're saving his life right now by keeping him from bleeding out."

"What you want from me, then?"

"I want you to enable his grid access. That way the race organizers or his support team will know he's in trouble. They'll come get his body, and you can keep going."

Marmeg shook her head. "Can't do."

"Why not? We'll make sure you still place. Don't worry about that."

"Can't. Not *won't*. Can't access zir cuff."

"But you're a hacker." Mountain Mike sounded confused.

"Not so easy. Could hack it, yeah, but takes time. Like hours time, not minutes time."

Mike blew out a frustrated breath and carefully sat down next to Ardha's body. She held a hand on zir wrist, checking zir pulse, Marmeg guessed. Then Mike felt Ardha's forehead and cheeks. She reached into a pocket, pulled out an old phone, and held it up to her head.

"His pulse is weak, and he's clammy," she said, speaking into the handset.

Marmeg could barely hear the words over the wind.

"Maybe another hour or so to live, best guess. Not long enough for her to run to the finish line and inform them." A pause. "No, that won't work. What story could she give them?" A longer pause, then louder: "Are you kidding? Just leave him here?"

Mike snapped the phone closed in anger and stood. "If you idiots didn't think you were invincible, you wouldn't get us into situations like this. Let's go!"

"What about zir?"

"We have to leave him. You need to win this race more than we need to help him. So says our leadership. He lives or dies on his support team. That's a risk all of you take, right? You sign the damn waivers when you enter."

"Nobody's ever died."

"Then he won't either. Now, come on!"

"No."

"What do you mean?"

"Not leaving zir. Not like this."

Mike flapped her arms like she was trying to fly off the mountain. "I thought you said you couldn't do anything?"

"Got my own grid access."

"You can't use that. Then we all lose. We'll get nothing for helping you, and once they realize you've been working with us, they'll ban you from races forever. Is that what you want?"

Marmeg was certainly happy to see Ardha lose the race after what zie had done to her. But to potentially let a person die over money? She would despise herself for it.

She'd pulled herself from the precipice of self-hatred once before, when the glow of being a prodigy had worn off. Marmeg had lived the high school party circuit for a year. Jeffy left for the service, and she had no one to remind her of her worth. Contest money that Amihan didn't take was burned on pills. Spare time—and she had plenty of that—was lost in the haze of self-loathing.

If she hadn't met T'shawn, if he hadn't remembered Marmeg from the old days, she might never have crawled out of her head hole and back into life. This race, the prize money, her dream future: none of these was worth the risk of returning to that ugly corner of her mind.

"Race not the be-all. Zie might die."

"I know. That's why I brought you here. Look, this situation is crap, but we have to put the greater good first. If you won't change your mind . . . well, I can't blame you, but I can't help you, either."

She turned and started walking up the scree.

"That's it?" Marmeg called after her. "Buncha nats think you're the stuff! Let a kid die on money? Some things not worth being."

Marmeg took out her screen, enabled her grid access, and sent a message to the race organizers. She took some photos of Ardha's situation, too—so they'd know what to bring—and sent a capture of her map with the GPS coordinates displayed. She made sure to disable her grid access again after seeing the send confirmation.

Minerva Corporation did good work. Maybe they'd be decent and not disqualify her for trying to save another contestant's life. They could check her system log for proof—she accessed the grid only to help Ardha.

"Better live, asshole," Marmeg whispered to the un-moving body. Ardha's face was beautiful in spite of its half-bloodied, pale state.

She stood, flexed her calves, and ran up the rocky slope. Pebbles flew behind her, drawn by gravity to whatever waited at the bottom. The Mike's figure was a shadow crawling along the scree and struggling for purchase. Marmeg continued her swift ascent without giving it a second look.

~

Marmeg got enough of a lead on Mountain Mike that she was well out of sight before taking her bearings. Once she had her location, she pulled up her original route. It was only two miles away, which wasn't bad considering how completely she had put herself in the hands of the Mikes.

The moon shone overhead. The clouds had fractured into patches of fluffy gray across the sky. Stars twinkled in the gaps, crystal clear even with the lunar glare for competition. Hundreds of diamond pinpoints—more than Marmeg had ever seen. Cold settled into her, a now-familiar friend, and her spirits lightened.

Win or lose, she'd made the only right decision. Losing wouldn't be so bad. Then she wouldn't have to share the contest money with people who valued an agenda over a human being. Or maybe they were only indifferent when an embed's life was at risk. What would they have said if it had been a Mike under the crush of rock? How many Mikes died out there with no one the wiser?

The land felt emptier with that last thought. Running into Ardha the first time had been a coincidence. If the Mountain Mikes hadn't sought her out, she might have finished the race without seeing anyone else. The lack of humanity was strange, like an empty street with no cop cars to explain it—wrong but not frightening.

Marmeg's cuff alerted her to the upcoming pass. This one would take her to the finish line. She found the trail marked by cairns and followed it up an uneven set of steps carved out of the granite mountainside. The footing wasn't difficult, but she chafed at having to climb the steps rather than simply leaping up them. That would have required functional thigh-control chips.

She walked between looming masses of rock. The faintest trace of purplish blue colored the eastern sky. She checked her cuff: three thirty in the morning. The sun would rise in two hours, but she would reach the finish line long before then.

The rushing noise of Rainbow Falls told her she was close. Next came fences made of rough wood to guide people and keep them on the trail, away from the cliff.

And then, at last, the striated columns of Devils Postpile rose into the sky. Artificial lights illuminated the natural formation, a beacon to the contestants: the end of the race.

The thrum of an electric generator greeted Marmeg as she loped into the staging area. She squinted against the flood of light triggered by her motion. Drone-cams perched on tree branches. The nearest ones launched and pointed their lenses at her. Zippered tents littered the area. Silhouettes stirred inside some of them, probably alerted by their drones.

Marmeg flicked on her cuff and saw that it was three minutes past four o'clock. She hadn't beaten the record. Apparently, no one else had either, given the lack of a welcoming committee. A shadowy figure emerged from the trees on the far side of the camp and walked toward her. Zie came into the lit area, and Marmeg recognized the blond moot from the registration booth.

"I'm so sorry," zie said. "I had to, you know, answer the call of nature. So, you're the first! Congratulations on winning this year's race!"

The drone-cams buzzed closer, recording and transmitting the conversation. Marmeg attempted a smile as they walked to a nondescript brown tent.

Zie unzipped the opening and called into it, "Jer, wake up! We have a winner."

Within minutes, all the tents had opened. People and drones spilled out into the darkness. Groggy journos snapped pictures of Marmeg. She waved away their questions while she ate an energy bar and huddled in a scratchy blanket someone handed her.

Meanwhile, the blond—whose name turned out to be Larlou—and Jer were rapidly setting up the official Minerva booth. Ten minutes after Marmeg's arrival, the second race contestant ran in. Keni Matsuki, last year's third-place winner, held an arm swathed in bloody smartsuit fabric. The medical team immediately looked to zir injury.

Marmeg's tired mind snapped to attention at the sight of blood.

"Hey, Larlou," she said. "Ardha—zie okay?"

Larlou looked up from the equipment rack.

"Who? What are you talking about?"

"Ardha! Sent you a message. Zie was hurt bad."

Larlou looked at Jer in bewilderment. "Did you hear about this from any of the support teams?"

"No," Jer said. He frowned and turned to Marmeg. "You said you pinged them?"

"Not them. You. Message to race org."

"Well, shit, kid, why didn't you inform zir support team?"

"Didn't know their address. Why didn't you get my

message?"

"I see it now," Larlou said. "Zie looks bad. We weren't expecting anything urgent, so we weren't looking at messages. I'll go find zir team's tent."

"Zie doesn't make it, it's on you."

She closed her eyes against a surge of frustration and fear. So much time had elapsed. What if they were too late? She had assumed that Ardha would be taken care of and gone by the time she arrived. Stupid and selfish not to ask about zir condition sooner.

"Wait a minute," Jer said.

Marmeg opened her heavy eyelids.

"You sent us a message. That means you accessed grid data."

She nodded. "Had to. Zie was unconscious. Couldn't access through zir cuff. Turned mine off after sending."

Jer's pale lips pressed into a thin line.

Marmeg's blood surged in anger. "What? Was I wrong? Leave zir to die out there?"

Her stomach sank at Jer's expression. They'd declared her the winner. Would they take it back? Could they? Most of her wanted nothing more than a hot shower and a soft bed, but her sense of justice couldn't rest. Minerva had to do the right thing, make the compassionate call. Didn't they?

Jer walked away, murmuring into his cuff. Dawn had

arrived in full effect. Marmeg could see his lips move, but she couldn't read the words. Adrenaline, pills, pain-induced endorphins: all of them crashed with the break of day. The energy to worry or rage evaporated. She collapsed into the blanket on the ground and fell asleep.

When she woke, rays of sunlight shone through the tree branches at a steep angle. Dust motes danced in the beams, and the aroma of frying eggs, bacon, and pancakes filled the air. She breathed in deeply and stretched. The cuts in her calves tugged uncomfortably, reminding Marmeg that she needed to see the medics.

The site swarmed with people. Contestants, supporters, and journos stood everywhere, eating and talking. Drone cameras buzzed in any available air space. Someone must have noticed that Marmeg was awake, because several cams moved to circle above her, swooping down to near face level and being annoying. Worse, three actual people surrounded her.

"How does it feel?" one of them asked.

"Congratulations! And condolences," said another. "For what it's worth, plenty of people on the grid think you did the right thing."

"What?" Marmeg said stupidly. Her brain felt like it was filled with wet beach sand.

The journos exchanged glances.

"You came in first place, but they've disqualified you

because you accessed the grid. Keni Matsuki is the official winner."

"Oh."

"Aren't you upset? It's looking very likely that you saved . . ." the journo checked zir cuff " . . . Ardhanara Jagadisha's life. People are already circulating a petition on your behalf to get Minerva to reinstate you as the winner."

"Oh. Thanks."

Marmeg walked past the baffled journos and over to the race tent.

"Truth?" she said to Larlou and Jer.

They looked at her apologetically.

"The race committee disqualified you, Mary. I'm so sorry," Larlou said. "I think you did the right thing, but they're saying that we can't know if you accessed any information or talked to someone who might have helped you while you were online."

Marmeg hadn't done either of those, but she had taken help from people off the grid. She had cheated. How could she justify defending the win?

"Look, kid," Jer said, "you did your best and you did great, but you should've hurried back here instead of turning on your access. We didn't know about Ardhanara until then anyway. Zie was alive when we picked zir up. Everyone knows the risk they're taking when they enter this race. Zie did too, and frankly, the route zie picked wasn't smart. What you did was noble, but it wasn't too smart, either."

"Jer!" Larlou protested. "Don't listen to him. If there's enough public outcry, Minerva will force the race committee to change its mind. It'll all come out right, Mary. You'll see. Have some faith."

Words bubbled into Marmeg's mind and floated away before she could speak. Was it better to confess the truth or play the wronged innocent? She had broken the rules—not the ones the race people knew about, but rules nonetheless. At least Ardha had survived. Marmeg hoped zie felt like an ass when zie found out who had saved zir.

"Is there anything we can do for you?" Larlou said. "Your support team never showed."

"That's because she doesn't have one," Jer said. His voice wasn't entirely unkind. "I bet I know what she needs."

Jer reached for Marmeg's cuff hand. She pulled it back by instinct.

"I'm going to transfer some credit," Jer said patiently. He looked sad. "I wish it had turned out differently, but this race is as much a publicity event for Minerva as it is any real test of ability. You handed them an excuse to keep you out of the winner's circle. They're going to take that as a gift."

Shame and anger welled in Marmeg until she wanted to scream. Instead, she thrust out her cuff while looking away at the treetops. She needed money to get home. Taking it from Jer was better than having to call Jeffy or her mother.

"Thanks," she mumbled, reactivating grid access on her screen so the transaction could complete.

The amount would cover bus fare and some frugal meals. Messages cascaded in as the cuff and screen re-discovered the rest of the world. Marmeg watched as the number ticked up and then jumped and then shot toward the moon. The cuff's buffer overflowed first, then her screen's. Marmeg muttered a curse she'd learned from Felix and Lee's father.

She searched the grounds for a speck of privacy to read them, but a few persistent drones wouldn't stop chasing her. She glared up at them.

"Did right!" she said loudly but not shouting.

If she was acting for the grid, she would rather play for sympathy. And she spoke the truth. Abandoning her message queue, she sat down in the middle of everything, activity swirling around her. She had yet to take off her gear.

Marmeg gritted her teeth against a groan when she pulled off the first calf exo. She couldn't help but wince.

Someone must have noticed, because a medic was on her by the time she had the second one off.

The medic took one look at her blood-crusted pants and motioned Marmeg to follow. Her legs were little better than jelly without the exos. She stumbled on nothing, and the medic reached out, supporting her by the elbow the rest of the way. Pitying looks accompanied them as they walked. The relative isolation of the tent provided her with much-needed privacy.

"What the hell did you do?" the medic demanded. "It looks like you cut yourself open with a kitchen knife."

"Near as much. Had to swap fried chips."

The medic looked horrified. "Out there? By yourself? With no sterilization or anesthesia? You're insane!" Zie shook zir head. "You're lucky you made it this long."

Zie kept muttering about infection and poisoning as zie readied a tray of gleaming instruments.

"Lie down," zie said. "On your stomach."

Marmeg yelped as chilly fingers pushed around her incisions.

"Oh, please. It must've hurt a lot more when you made these incisions. I can see quite a bit of swelling here, but the wound is closed. We're better off leaving it alone. I'm going to take some blood samples to check for infection."

Marmeg craned her head and watched the medic

draw a vial of blood. Zie placed a few drops into a row of cylinders the size of her thumb. After a minute, zie scanned each one with a handheld and frowned at the screen. Marmeg held her breath until the medic's face relaxed.

"Lucky girl. Your blood is clear of sepsis. You do have a mild infection, which is hardly unexpected, but it's nothing a course of antibiotics won't clear up. I'm going to get them from the supply box outside. Stay put."

Marmeg sat up. The world spun. She debated getting a few more stim pills from her backpack, but the medic returned before she'd moved. Zie carried a blister pack of antibiotics and a bottle of water.

"Take two now and another one every twelve hours until they're all gone. And no more stimulants." Had zie read her mind? "You need to let your body rest and recover. Get lots of sleep, drink plenty of water, and take it easy on the legs for at least a week. No exos! I recommend seeing a surgeon at that point to reopen your calves and check the capsule placement. They might be able to reduce the scarring, too. As it is now, you're going to end up with some ugly ones."

Marmeg sighed and took the first dose. The giant, bitter pills stuck in her throat, and she drank nearly half the bottle before she swallowed them.

"Thanks."

"You're welcome. I'm sorry about the race."

"Same."

She shouldered her pack and brought up her planned return route on her cuff. A free shuttle would get her to Mammoth Lakes. From there she could catch the bus to Los Angeles.

A winding cement path led to a rectangular building and the signpost for the shuttle. There was nowhere to sit while waiting, so Marmeg dropped her pack on the pavement and slumped beside it. Two journo drones had trailed her, but they lost interest once she stopped moving. She had thirty minutes until the next shuttle. In her sleep-deprived state, it felt like an eternity.

The bus pulled in with a squeal of brakes that woke her from a light doze. A couple and two young children got down, and Marmeg climbed on. She took up two seats, one for herself and another for the pack, but it didn't matter. The bus was empty except for her.

She dozed off again, rousing only when the driver informed her that they'd arrived in town. She could smell toasted bread as she stepped off. Her stomach growled. Marmeg entered the bakery from which all the lovely, mouth-watering odors came, and ordered a bagel, toast with fried eggs, and a pitcher of orange juice. It would make a sizeable dent in the money Jer had given her.

She sat at a table in the back corner, though there was

no one to hide from except the server. The food arrived steaming. It was the most delectable meal of Marmeg's life, and she devoured it at a pace that barely allowed for chewing and swallowing.

"Glad you enjoyed your meal," the server said as zie cleared the dishes away.

"Best ever." Marmeg held up her cuff to pay.

"No charge."

"What?"

The server smiled. "Most everyone here follows the race. A free breakfast is the least I can do."

"Thanks."

Win or lose, fame had its benefits. Marmeg made sure to bump the server's and the bakery's ratings on her way out.

The bus terminal in town was small, but it was enclosed and clean, and had padded seats. Marmeg slept until her cuff zapped her awake. Time to catch the bus. She blearily joined the handful of others getting on. The driver stopped her when she held her cuffed wrist to the credit scanner.

"Sorry, cash only today. Scanner's broken."

"Jokin'?"

The driver shook his head. "There's a cash dispenser inside. I'll wait for you."

Marmeg kept her pack with her and limped back into

the station. She swiped her cuff three times at the machine to no effect. Then she noticed the small card with OUT OF ORDER scribbled in red and taped to the top.

"My God, why hast thou forsaken me?" she muttered, feeling a strong urge to kick the machine.

She walked back out and asked the driver if he knew of any other machines nearby. He didn't. When was the next bus? Not for two more days. His face crinkled with pity.

"I'll make you a deal," he said. "Show me the credit balance on your cuff. If it's enough, I'll give you a ride. You can get me some cash at the next station."

"Deal," Marmeg agreed.

She sat and put the pack vertically next to herself. She leaned against it like an old friend and fell into a deep sleep. In her dreams, towering trees tangled with walls of granite. Rocks crashed through them, creating an avalanche of roots and soil and mangled, screaming bodies.

"Hey," said a gentle voice. "Got to wake up here and get your bus fare."

Marmeg awoke disoriented and stared at the owner of the voice: a graying man with asphalt-colored skin. Right. She was on a bus, nearly out of money, and going home a cheat and a failure. *You're wrong, Ma. God doesn't love me.*

Every muscle ached and every joint protested when she stood and pulled on the pack. The first four steps along the bus aisle were pure agony. Then blood pulsed its way to the right places, including her brain. She wondered where they were until she saw the sign proclaiming RIDGECREST in faded green lettering. The cash machine looked even worse. At least it dispensed.

Marmeg was tempted by the smell of coffee but decided it would be smarter to sleep. She thought of all the messages on her cuff. At the very least, she owed a note to Jeffy that she'd made it onto the bus in one piece. Then again, if the race news kept topping the feeds, he would know enough.

"Hoy. You Mary Guinto, right? Graf me?" said a voice from behind her.

She turned and saw two kids, probably thirteen or fourteen years old. One had her screen thrust out at Marmeg. Her face had a shy, nervous expression that felt all too familiar.

"Lost the race."

"Won it, squares!" said the kid fiercely. "They gone it 'cause of who you be, but we all know you done first."

Marmeg smiled at her defenders. "Okay. I'll graf."

She scribbled a message next to her signature: TO MY FIRST FANS. Her pack felt a little lighter on her way back to the bus.

Marmeg's cuff bleated as she took her seat. She flicked it on. The backlog had grown. One after another, messages scrolled by. The earliest were congratulatory. They became supportive, then outraged. Petitions against Minerva's race committee were filed. Many protested that it was blatant discrimination against a postnatal licensee. Others were appalled by Minerva's inhumanity.

Hours' worth of drama played out in the space of a few minutes. Her ratings had soared, dipped, risen, and dipped again. They had acquired a life of their own.

She set her cuff not to wake her until the bus arrived in Los Angeles. Of the rest of the journey, she remembered nothing, not even her dreams.

~

Marmeg felt more like herself when she stepped off the bus at the dingy LA station. A gentle mist fell from a cement-colored sky. The sun had set, painting the west an angry orange.

She walked past the lot full of two-seater pods and older electric cars, intending to foot it to the nearest train station. The sight of her family's rusty electric minivan caught her off guard. Dirty beads of water trickled down its side windows. Marmeg peered in and saw with a sinking heart that her mother sat at the wheel. The window glass retracted jerkily into the door.

"Come in out of the rain, mahal."

Marmeg slung her pack into the middle row and climbed into the passenger seat.

"How'd you know?"

"Oh, honey, you are all over the feeds. I made Jeffy tell me how you were planning to get home, so I've been waiting here. I'm off today."

"Ma, that's . . . real nice of you. Thanks."

Amihan patted Marmeg's left hand. "Least I could do for my girl after all she's put herself through."

"No stink?"

"No stink. I'm not mad at you. Everybody makes mistakes. Lord knows, I get that better than most, eh?" Amihan laughed. "Sometimes, we have to learn the hard way, us women, especially in our family."

The wiper blades squeaked, and the scent of stale tobacco filled the car. Marmeg's comfort at being home warred with her mother's unexpected sympathy. When added to everything else that had happened in the past twenty-four hours, the whole world felt off-kilter.

She stared through the window at a city turned upside down by a hundred perfect water drops. She was a snowflake poised on a warm tongue, awaiting its inevitable death and cherishing the memory of its brief, spectacular life.

Reality crashed in: familiar shop fronts with peeling paint and screen signs with half their pixels gone. This part of the neighborhood was etched into Marmeg's memory as clearly as traces on a circuit board.

"What we doing here?"

Amihan kept her gaze fixed on the wet, shiny blackness of the road.

"Ma? Talk to me!"

Her mother pulled into a cracked, weed-choked driveway alongside an industrial-looking building. CASA FRANCISCA WOMEN'S SHELTER: the sign hung on the wall in dull metal letters. Amihan turned off the car's engine.

"Tell me the truth. Did you register and pay for the nursing home program?"

"No."

"Did you spend that money on the race?"

"It's my money."

"Did you?"

"Yes."

"Thank you for being honest. Tonight, I'm going to take you home. Your brothers have planned a little party, and I don't want to disappoint them. Tomorrow morning, you can come here on your own, or I'll drop you off on the way to work. You will not be welcome at home again until you figure out how to fix this mess."

"Fix it your way?"

"Seems better than yours."

"I won the race!"

"And they took it away from you, like I knew they would. You think because you're smart, you can engineer your way into their life, but you'll never be one of them. They don't want people like us messing up their perfect circles."

Marmeg crossed her arms, restrained herself against the urge to smash something. Anything.

Amihan reached out a tentative hand. "Take your hardships with grace, Mary Margaret. God is testing you! This is your chance to earn His forgiveness."

"And yours?"

"Mine comes through His grace. I'm your mother, so I'll always love you, but I won't sit by and watch my daughter destroy her life. Are we clear?"

"Crystal."

Amihan backed out of the driveway. They drove to the apartment in silence and left the van parked between a two-seater and an ancient gas-burner. The mist had turned to actual falling drops of rain. They hurried inside, where they were surprised by two boys in handmade party hats. A sign reading WELCOME HOME SISSY was written in wiggly lettering.

"Surprise!" shouted Lee and Felix, jumping up and down with giant grins plastered on their faces.

Marmeg forced a smile. She dropped her pack near the door and scooped her little brothers into a tight hug. Felix's sweet curls tickled her chin.

"Best brothers in the world," she exclaimed, fighting tears.

"Hey, what about me?" Jeffy said, walking into the apartment.

Marmeg turned and gave Jeffy the next hug. His stubbly cheeks were cold and damp, and he held a bottle in each hand.

"Wine, Jeffy?" Amihan spoke in an appraising tone. She took the bottles from him and peered at the labels. "This one's not bad," she said. She walked to the kitchen and grabbed the corkscrew that lay on the countertop. The surface was so littered with pans and dishes that Marmeg could barely see the yellowing, cracked tiles underneath.

Amihan poured the wine into plastic cups and handed one each to Marmeg and Jeffy. She grabbed cans of soda from the fridge for Lee and Felix. Little eyes went wide.

"I get a whole can?" Felix squeaked.

"Sure, baby. We're celebrating!" Amihan said.

"We are? I got the wine to make Marm feel better for

losing the race."

"Jeffy! No, we're celebrating that Mary is coming to her senses and quitting this embed nonsense."

Jeffy and Felix simultaneously said, "She is?"

Jeffy looked at Marmeg for confirmation, and she shrugged. His face darkened.

"No way, Ma. We can't let her quit. She won! Do you know how hard that is?"

"But she didn't keep the win, and she threw away her future in the process."

"Are you saying she should've let that person die?"

"Of course not, Jeffy. What do you take me for?"

"Enough! Too tired to fight this tonight," Marmeg said. "Sort it in daylight, brud, okay?" She raised her cup toward Jeffy, who glowered but raised his as well. "To new beginnings."

The first sip of wine left Marmeg's tongue coated in acid. The next slurp was as cool and sweet as a mountain stream. Whether or not she had deserved any of it—Ardha's sabotage, the Mikes' help, the disqualification—it didn't matter anymore. Nobody in real life got what they deserved. At least Marmeg had been spared the self-loathing she would've felt for winning by cheating.

Who was she kidding? She desperately wanted all of that success. She wanted to be out there, under the trees and the shadow of mountains, getting interviewed by journos and fending off sponsors and rabid fan requests. Instead, she stuffed some basics into her pack while the boys jumped away their soda high. Jeffy and their mother were too drunk to notice.

The celebration didn't last long. The younger boys sugar-crashed and turned in. Jeffy fell asleep on the sofa, and Amihan wept at the kitchen table about her ill-fated family until she passed out with her head on her arms.

Marmeg slung the pack over her shoulder. She stood by the door and took in the tableau. Better to leave now than face the drama of the morning. She ducked out and closed the door. The chill, moist air was a welcome relief after the stuffiness of their apartment. The rain had tapered into a heavy mist that clung to Marmeg and slicked the sidewalk. Fog blew in ghostly drifts from the coast and wove around the street lights.

A quarter of the distance passed before her calves protested. Too late she recalled the medic's warning to stay off her legs. She gritted her teeth against the pain, but she was limping badly by the time she arrived at the shelter.

"I'm sorry I don't have a bed for you," said the night manager. She handed Marmeg a ratty sleeping bag. "The rain's got us full tonight. You're welcome to find a spot on the floor."

Marmeg found an empty space by the wall of a cavernous room lined with bunk beds, all occupied. She settled her pack behind her, trying to get the softer items to provide some cushion from the gear. Somewhere on the other side of the wall, a baby wailed. Marmeg slid her legs into the bag, shoes and all, and leaned back to check her ratings.

Minerva had released a statement saying they would look into the Sierra Challenge results, but as of yet, they hadn't contacted Marmeg even once. The only people who had reached out to her were others in similar situations: born without a license, filching their gear, stuck in dead-end jobs that didn't require legit schooling—the people for whom she embodied hope.

Her ratings bounded around like a demented basketball. She sighed as she cleared the cuff's message buffer again and again. In the final cluster of private messages was one from Jeffy: MOM'S WAITING AT BUS STATION FOR YOU. Too bad she hadn't seen the warning earlier. Then, near the end of the list, a one-liner from a meaningless address: SILENCE IS GOLDEN.

So, the Mountain Mikes were paying attention. Was that a promise? A threat? Did it matter? She had given them her answer already.

She lay awake for a long time and stared at the cement ceiling. Salty, unshed tears ran down the back of her throat, draining away like her dreams. A real degree, embed races, moot surgery: all gone. Hope receded to an unreachable distance in the hours after midnight.

The restless murmurs and snuffles of slumbering bodies surrounded her. She had to get herself out of the shelter, but how? Sleep took her at last, before she came up with a good answer.

~

The morning bell rang. Gray daylight filtered in through high, small windows. The room came to life with yawns and groans and the creak of metal frames. Marmeg left the shelter after eating breakfast. She needed fresh air.

Last night's rain had left the city smelling earthy and clean. She walked to a dilapidated park bench and sat down to check her messages.

She had a new one from T'shawn: MINERVA RACE COMM SAY RULES BE RULES. FANS BE FIGHTING BACK. His earlier message—the one he'd sent at the start of the race—caught her attention: GIVE ME YOUR GEAR IF YOU TOAST OUT?

He'd meant it as a joke, but she *had* almost toasted out. The words nagged at her mind. Her gear: exos, chips, sleeves. They would be worth something. She felt sick at the thought, but she couldn't conceive of a better solution. The shelter would give her two weeks. After that, she'd be out on the street with no address. Her ratings would plummet. No one would employ her. The sooner she could get back home, the better.

MEET UP AT ELEVEN-OH? she sent to T'shawn.

He responded that he could. She spent the morning answering what passed for fan mail, not that she had any prior experience to go by. Half of it was hateful—the usual rants against unlicensed and postnatals freeloading off taxpayers—and the other half exhorted her to fight Minerva. DON'T LET THEM DENY YOU! BE THE HERO WE NEED! But in her heart, she couldn't be what they wanted, not with this race. Not until she won by her own means.

The walk to T'shawn's place took ten times longer than it would have with functional calf muscles. She limped past cars for hire that she couldn't afford. Her mind jittered with lingering frustration, and her whole body ached, but her mood lifted when she entered the abandoned building where her friend lived and worked.

He was holed up in a back room, well hidden from the street by small, paper-covered windows. Black-market gear gleamed in stacks around the perimeter. A workbench sat against the far wall. An oscilloscope, multimeters, probes, and screens littered its surface.

T'shawn gave her a rueful smile, grasped her shoulder

in a half hug.

"Win some, lose some," he said.

"Full right, that."

"What you be here for today? Twice in a week is a special treat." He flashed his toothy grin at her.

"Want a quiet talk for a sell-back."

His grin vanished. "Marm, you not serious. What you do with yourself if you go back to nat? Don't let this race bull get you lost in the head, friend."

"Only way out, brud," Marmeg said. "Get good credit for all my chips. Pay out school fees. Do the slow way."

"Old way, more like," he said, grimacing.

"Yeah, well, Ma kicked me out. Stuck myself good."

"Not again!"

Marmeg pressed the case with the two unused chips into T'shawn's hand.

"How much for these plus the seven inside? Three of 'em busted."

T'shawn sucked on his upper lip as he typed in some numbers. He showed her the final tally on his screen.

"Minus a few hundred for the surgeon."

It would be enough to cover the first tuition installment for the elder care program—enough to get her back into Amihan's good graces.

"Trigger it. Set me up with the doc. Got any work for me?"

"Naw, Marm, nothing paid. Barely cover my own. Get me some new code, might get you some treats again."

"Can't test code without chips."

"Don't give up, hear? You one of the best we ever got, and you need to get out. Show the kids what can do. Get me a benefits gig someday."

Marmeg laughed to cover the lump in her throat. "Stay sane, brud. Ping me when you got the date."

~

Her next stop was a used-gear shop. She'd filched many of her own exos from the trash cans in the back. The owner didn't mind, since he couldn't fix the broken stuff, and he would buy some of Marmeg's flips when she found an upgrade. The inside of the store was crammed with floor-to-ceiling shelves. Dusty plastic bins brimmed with parts sorted by function.

Marmeg walked along the scuffed, dirty floor tiles and went straight to the front counter. Chips gleamed inside the glass case. She put her bag of gear down, fighting the urge to curse at the tiny capsules. The sound of clanking metal drew the owner from the back. His tight gray curls contrasted with his dark skin, and his face crinkled into a broad smile.

"Marmeg! What can I do for you?"

She marveled that he remembered her name. She couldn't recall his. He'd tolerated her filching, but he hadn't been this friendly in the past.

"Want to sell this."

"Sure, sure. You must be in line for some real gear now." He sorted through the items, putting the torn and bloody sleeve straight into the trash, separating the older-generation parts from the new.

"No more gear. I'm out."

"But the race—you can't be quitting now?"

So, he knew about that. "Full busted. Race took the last of it, and Mom kicked me out. Need money."

He pushed the gear aside and leaned on the counter. "Well that's a shame, considering your skills. I thought a scout would've picked you up by now, got you some sponsors."

She shook her head.

"Have you seen your ratings? The news today? You're up. Minerva's sinking like a rock."

Marmeg shrugged. Ratings had their value, but they didn't pay for tuition or put food on the table.

The shop owner sighed. "This stuff isn't worth much. How about a job? You fix broken gear for me, I pay you by the hour. And you have to work here, in the front, and record some ads for the store. Help me boost my ratings."

A job would let her save up, get Felix his license.

Maybe earn back her chips if she kept at it long enough. *What for?* she thought. *You'll never race again. They won't let you.* Regardless, she could use the money for any number of things, not the least of which was keeping Amihan off her back.

"Okay. Deal. Gotta sort some other business. Start next week?"

"I'll see you on Monday."

As Marmeg exited the shop, her cuff zapped her wrist. T'shawn had a surgery scheduled for her the following day.

~

Marmeg sat at a plastic table and ate a basket of hot, greasy fries with the last of Jer's credit. It was a treat to herself. Her legs and arms ached from the chip extractions, and pain pills were the only thing saving her from a stunning nitrous-oxide headache. She'd kept the chip in her brain stem. The surgeon wanted extra fees for that, and T'shawn had talked his buyer into a better price overall. It made little difference to keep it.

She traced the table's random cracks and stains with her left pinky. The heat from the fries soothed her raw throat. She'd managed to save her tears until she was alone. When she had let them loose, the sobs had ripped through her like an angry spirit. She needed the comfort of starch and fat.

Her cuff buzzed, and Marmeg looked down to see a stranger requesting a live call. The face belonged to an older man with lined brown skin, dark eyes, and wire-rimmed glasses. A full beard and moustache matched his salt-and-pepper hair. She accepted the call.

"Miss Guinto, yes? I'm sorry to bother you like this. My name is Sachiv Jagadisha."

Marmeg stared at him blankly. The name sounded familiar, but she couldn't recall why.

"I'm Ardha's father," he explained. "I'm calling you because I discovered that not only do we need to thank you for helping our child, we need to apologize for zir behavior. Ardha was gravely injured, and zie has been unconscious until today. They can't save zir natural legs, but zie is lucky to have so many enhancements already. They say they can integrate artificial muscle and bone into what's left."

Marmeg nodded, unsure how to respond. At least now she knew why the name and face were familiar. She could see the family resemblance.

"I'm sorry. I'm talking on and on. My child became lucid only yesterday. Zie confessed to my wife—zir mother—what zie had done to you earlier in the race. And yet you were kind enough to save zir at the cost of the race itself. You are truly selfless, and you have been very badly rewarded. My family and my colleagues who supported Ardha in the race—we would like to extend a credit to you."

"Can't take it."

"Please, you must. It's not a great deal of credit, but we feel badly about what our child has done."

Marmeg forced herself to speak in slow, full sentences. "Can't take it, sir, but thank you." She took a deep breath and decided she might as well tell him the whole truth; a confession for a confession. "I didn't win the race fairly. Got help from some . . . mountain people who took me to shortcuts. One of them brought me to Ardha, else I never would've found zir. And then—" She broke off, looked away from the kind brown eyes on the screen, and lapsed into familiar rhythms. "Did what was right. Tried to make up for cheats, you know?"

Ardha's father sighed. "You were sabotaged and you were aided, but that was the work of others. It is you who saved our child. Forget the race and think of the credit as a token of our gratitude. Please. My wife will not forgive me if I accept your refusal."

Marmeg's face flushed with suppressed tears. *Don't be an idiot. This money can only help, and why shouldn't you get something for all that you went through?* But the thought didn't sit right. A different idea nibbled around the edges of her mind.

"You got any pay gigs?"

"Sorry?"

"Paid work. A job I could do," Marmeg clarified. "Got a college admit but can't pay for it. That's partly why I raced. Want to get an embed design degree. Get myself out of this hole. Make a better life, you know? I can code for you."

"I see."

Sachiv's expression was distant, and Marmeg wondered if she'd blown her chance. Her school contests were too far in the past to count, but she had her own designs, the illegal ones.

"Custom built the 'ware for my own rig." She pulled her screen from her cargo pocket and sent him the source code. "Take a look. Steady pay beats a credit dump, you catch me?"

Sachiv smiled at her. "Quite right. Yes, quite right. Unfortunately, we cannot hire you until you have at least the bachelor's degree. Let me think about it some more. Perhaps I can find a happy solution. I'll get back to you."

The call ended. Marmeg leaned back against the hard curve of the seat. She looked around at an unfamiliar world, noise buzzing around her. Her heart raced and her hands shook as she took a bite of the fries. They were cold. She couldn't care. Her fate stood poised on a pinnacle, its balance as precarious as her footing during the race. Which way would it land?

Marmeg dumped the unappetizing food in the compost bin and walked outside. A hot, dry breeze whispered through her hair as she strolled along the uneven cement sidewalk and waited for the call. And walked. And waited some more. Sweat itched on the back of her neck. The afternoon wore on and the sun beat down from a cloudless sky, but sitting still proved impossible.

She was gulping water from a tepid public fountain when her cuff zapped. The message came from Ardha's father, all text: NO JOB OFFER. SORRY! BUT WE CAN PAY TUITION AND IF YOU KEEP UP YOUR GRADES, YOU'LL HAVE A REMOTE INTERNSHIP OFFER FOR NEXT SUMMER.

Marmeg didn't know whether to laugh or cry, so she sat on the sidewalk and did both. Getting a fully paid college education was monumental. Even her mother couldn't deny that. She could save all her money from the job at the used gear shop. Get her chips back. Get Felix's license. Race again next summer. She could go home.

She sent a reply to Ardha's dad with an electronic signature and the address to her empty credit account. Marmeg's mind reeled as she limped her way back to the shelter to collect her bag. In a few weeks, she'd be a college freshman, surrounded by hordes of licensed, well-groomed kids who took for granted three meals and a bed and hot showers. Life was about to get real different.

A half-dead pine tree grew in the empty lot to her left. She recalled the scent of alpine air and melting snowflakes, of cold stone tunnels and wet earth, and she hatched a plan: for another year, another race. She would win on her own merits. Trap the Mountain Mikes into revealing their hand. But most of all, she wanted to dance like the wind over granite mountaintops.

About the Author

Photograph by Susan Yoon

S. B. DIVYA is a lover of science, math, fiction, and the Oxford comma. She enjoys subverting expectations and breaking stereotypes whenever she can. In her past, she's used a telescope to find the Orion nebula, scuba dived with manta rays, and climbed to the top of a thousand-year-old stupa. You can find more of her writing at www.eff-words.com.

TOR·COM

Science fiction. Fantasy. The universe.

And related subjects.

*

More than just a publisher's website, *Tor.com*

is a venue for **original fiction, comics,** and

discussion of the entire field of SF and fantasy,

in all media and from all sources. Visit our site

today—and join the conversation yourself.